FREDDY

GOES CAMPING

Freddy's first one flew up into a tree.

FREDDY
GOES
CAMPING

by WALTER R. BROOKS

Illustrated by Kurt Wiese

NEW YORK · ALFRED · A · KNOPF

Introduction copyright © 1986 by Michael Cart. Cover illustration copy-right © 1986 by Leslie Morrill. Copyright 1948 by Walter R. Brooks. Copyright renewed 1975. All rights reserved under International and Pan-American Copyright Conventions. Published in the United States by Alfred A. Knopf, Inc., New York, and simultaneously in Canada by Ran-dom House of Canada Limited, Toronto. Distributed by Random House, Inc., New York. Originally published by Alfred A. Knopf, Inc., New York, in 1948.

The Library of Congress cataloged the first printing of this title as follows: Brooks, Walter Rollin, 1886–1958. Freddy goes camping; illus. by Kurt Wiese. [1st ed.] New York, A. A. Knopf, 1948.   I. Title.   PZ10.3.B76Fo 48-8629
ISBN 0-394-87602-4   ISBN 0-394-97602-9 (lib. bdg.)

Manufactured in the United States of America
2   4   6   8   10   9   7   5   3   1

Introduction

My best friend when I was growing up was Freddy the Pig, four of whose adventures Alfred A. Knopf has now republished. It took more than two dozen books to chronicle all of Freddy's adventures, though, for he was a prodigy: a pig of many parts. In these books, for example, you will meet him as politician, camper, pilot, balloonist, detective, poet, newspaper editor, and sportsman—uh, sports*pig*. Yet the one constant role he *never* failed to play was that of friend.

And it is the recurring theme of friendship warmly informing all of the Freddy books which elevates them to the status of American classics. When I was growing up, my friend Freddy taught me about the joys—and responsibilities—of friendship: of sharing and caring, of loyalty and constancy, of kindness, compassion, and forgiveness, and above all—of *helping*. Freddy's friends were often in danger; yet, even if Freddy was so frightened that his tail was completely uncurled, he gritted his teeth and did whatever was necessary to help. Growing up with the Freddy books, I learned a whole system of traditional values and enduring ethics.

Don't think for a minute that this means the books are preachy or moralistic or dull. On the contrary, they're exciting and unfailingly *funny*! The Freddy books are full of word play—of funny names and outrageous puns and amusing dialogue. Slapstick and satire are here, too, but the best of the books' humor arises out of the characters—out of Jinx the cat and Mrs. Wiggins the cow and Charles the rooster and others too numerous to mention, not only on the farm but also in Boomschmidt's Stupendous and Unexcelled Circus. Our friendship with these characters entitles us to laugh not *at* them but *with* them.

Finally, the Freddy books capture and preserve a uniquely American moment. Upstate New York is their setting, but they really belong to your hometown and mine, places that endure forever in our hearts.

You bet they're classics.

And my friend is a classic too. Welcome back, Freddy. You've been gone too long.

Michael Cart
City Librarian
Beverly Hills, California

FREDDY

GOES CAMPING

Chapter 1

The pigpen on the Bean farm stood a little above the barnyard. On the door was a small brass plate which said: Frederick Bean, Esq. Above the door was a sign:

Frederick & Wiggins
Detectives
Office hours: Wednesdays, 2-4 P.M.

To the left of the door was another sign:

Subscriptions taken here for
THE BEAN HOME NEWS
The animals' own newspaper.

This was the outside of the pigpen. Inside, sitting in his broken-down old armchair before his desk, was Freddy. Freddy, the pig: editor, poet, banker, detective. Today being Thursday, he was Freddy the editor, and he was getting the material in shape for the next issue of the paper. He had almost enough now; there was just one blank space left to fill. A small poem would just fit it. So he leaned on his left elbow and put his left front trotter to his brow and thus became Freddy the poet, waiting for inspiration.

So he waited. Every now and then he would lick his pencil. He had licked it so often that there was a black line right around his mouth. But there still wasn't a black mark on the blank leaf of his notebook where the poem was supposed to be. And there was a knock at the door.

"Rats!" said Freddy. Then he called impatiently: "Come in!"

The door flew open and a short red-faced man with rather loud clothes and a bristly mustache came in.

"Mr. Camphor!" Freddy exclaimed.

"Jimson to you, my boy, always," said the man.

They shook hands and Freddy said: "Well,

Mr.—er, Jimson, do sit down. It's pretty nice of you to come see me. Of course if I'd known you were coming I'd have tidied up a little. Hate to have you see the place in such a mess."

Mr. Camphor glanced around. Papers were piled on the desk and overflowed onto the floor. Freddy hadn't had time to make his bed, or clear away his breakfast dishes, and the only other chair in the room was heaped nearly as high as the desk. "I'd have had to give you about three days' notice, I guess," Mr. Camphor said with a laugh, "and I wouldn't want you to go to all that trouble on my account. Anyhow, I can't stop. Got to get back to see what Aunt Minerva is up to."

"I didn't know you had an aunt," Freddy said.

"Goodness, everybody has aunts. I've got two. I've made quite a study of aunts. There's two kinds: there's the regular kind, and then there's the other kind. Mine are the other kind. You'll see when you meet 'em."

"Meet them?" said Freddy. "They're here?"

"Oh, no. See here, Freddy." Mr. Camphor sat down on the edge of the bed. "I need your help. I want you to . . ." He stopped. "No, better not tell you till you've seen them. See here. Can't you bring your partner and come up for a few days? Look the ground over; see what can be done. Eh? You've been promising to pay me a visit for a year. How about it?"

"Why, I could," said Freddy. "Sure, we'll come. But what is it you want me to do?"

"I'll tell you *what*," said Mr. Camphor, getting up, "but there's no time to tell you *why*. I want you to get rid of my aunts."

"Good gracious!" said Freddy. "You mean . . . ?"

"Oh, no—not kidnap them or push them in the lake or anything," said Mr. Camphor with a laugh. "Get them to leave—that's all. Ha, think it over. And I'll expect you and Mrs. Wiggins tomorrow, eh?" He was gone before Freddy could ask another question.

Freddy hurried after him. At least he tried to, but the springs of his old chair were broken so that he was sitting almost on the floor, and he had to be specially careful because the ends of some of them stuck through the upholstery. If you moved too quickly, they jabbed you. By the time Freddy got outside, Mr. Camphor's car was rolling out of the Bean gate.

Freddy realized that his guest had been

pretty smart. "He's told me just enough to make me want to know more," he thought. "He knows that's the way to get us up there." But he would have been glad to go in any case. For he had been the caretaker last summer on Mr. Camphor's big estate, and they had become fast friends.

Sitting on the roof of the pigpen was Mr. J. J. Pomeroy. Mr. Pomeroy was a robin, and he was the messenger who would fly Freddy's manuscript down to the printing office in Centerboro, when Freddy had it ready. He was hopping up and down with impatience. "For goodness' *sake*, Freddy," he said, "hurry up! I want to get back home before dark. You know I don't like night flying since I've been wearing glasses." Mr. Pomeroy was nearsighted, and had had a lot of trouble until Freddy had taken him to an optician and had a little pair of spectacles made for him.

"Oh, do shut up," said Freddy crossly. "If I could think of something I was interested in enough to write about, I'd be through in . . . What are *you* interested in, J.J.?" he asked, looking up at the robin.

Mr. Pomeroy lifted a claw and took off his

glasses and polished them on his wing. "Why, let me see," he said. "My wife and family, of course. After that—why, I guess I'd say, worms."

"Worms," said Freddy thoughtfully. "I've never written a poem about worms. Not much to say about them, as far as I can see."

"That's where you're wrong," said the robin. "Worms are one of the first subjects we robins teach our children about. Why worms, my dear sir, are the staff of life! Do you realize that there are more than two thousand edible varieties in the United States alone?"

"Ugh! That's an awful thought," said Freddy with a shudder. "An incredible thought— hey, wait a minute!" He ran in and brought out his notebook.

"Of course," Mr. Pomeroy went on, "some kinds are better than others, if you know what I mean."

"You mean 'worse' instead of 'better' don't you?" Freddy looked up from what he was writing.

"Not at all. Better. Deliciouser. For my money one of those small, light green inch worms—what you call a measuring worm; you know the kind—he has some feet in front, and then for quite a long distance he's just worm, and then at the back end there are some more feet. So when he walks, he stretches out and puts down his front feet, and then brings his back feet up close to them so that his body makes a kind of loop. Very handy to pick them up by. They're really very tasty, Freddy. So crisp and tender! Let me find you one, and you just try it once, will you?"

"Not for a million dollars!" said Freddy. "It makes my stomach flutter just to think of it. Listen, J.J.; how's this?"

But before he could start to read, Jinx, the cat, came running up. "Hi, pig; how's the old inspiration this morning—hitting on all six?"

"Go away," said Freddy. "I'm busy."

"What's that black lipstick you've got on—some new fashion you're starting?" Jinx asked. "Hey," he said, "don't throw anything! I just came over to tell you there's a chipmunk here to see you. Got a message for you—he won't tell us what it is. He's over at the barn."

"Well, I can't come now," said Freddy. "Tell him to wait. I'll be over in a little while."

"OK, I'll tell him you'll be over when you get your make-up on." And Jinx sauntered off.

"Smart aleck!" Freddy growled. "Well now, listen, J.J." And he read:

"To say that worms are edible
Will seem to you incredible.
For you to eat a measuring worm
Would take more courage and determ-
*   ination than to take a dive i-*
*   nto a clump of poison ivy*
Yet robins eat them every day;
They smack their beaks and shout Hooray!
They gobble them with joy and pride
And do not seem upset inside."

"It doesn't get anywhere," said the robin.

"No," said the pig; "that's true. There's no moral. Unless . . ." He wrote again for a minute. "How's this?"

"The moral here is plain to see:
What pleases you does not please me;
What pleases me to you is hateful,
And for this fact we should be grate—"

"Look, Freddy," Mr. Pomeroy interrupted. "You want me to be quite frank, don't you?"

"Of course," said Freddy. "Of course, my dear chap. An honest opinion is worth more than all the flattery in the world."

"OK, then," said Mr. Pomeroy. "I think it's just plain dull. Everybody knows that if we all

"Hi, pig; how's the old inspiration this morning?"

liked the same thing, there wouldn't be enough to go round."

Now when people say they want an honest opinion about something they've done, they probably mean it all right, but if it isn't a favorable opinion, they're apt to get mad.

"So what?" said Freddy crossly. "You're so smart—suppose you write it."

"Why not?" said Mr. Pomeroy. He thought a minute. Then he said:

"To say that worms are edible may seem to you incredible,
  And yet I most emphatically assert
That hardly any dishes are more filling or deliciouser
  Than angleworms pulled freshly from the dirt."

"H'm," said the pig. "Not bad, not bad at all for a first effort. I might sign your name to it. How would you go on from there?"

"Well, I'd go on to other kinds—plan a well-balanced meal, do you see? Beetles, flies, and then maybe go into caterpillars . . ."

"No," Freddy said. "No. Our readers aren't squeamish specially, but I doubt if they'd care for a description of a complete bug dinner.

Tell you what I'll do, J.J. I'll print that verse, and take up the rest of the space with a little note: With the following deft and original verse, our esteemed fellow citizen, Mr. J.J. Pomeroy, makes his debut as a full-fledged poet in this issue. Possessing a degree of technical skill unusual in a beginner—and so on and so on. How about it?"

Mr. Pomeroy was delighted and as soon as Freddy had written it out, he took the paper and flew off to Centerboro. Freddy was pleased, too. His own verses, he knew, weren't much good. "My goodness," people would say when they read them, "Freddy is slipping." Of course the robin's weren't very good either. But nobody would criticize Freddy for them.

When Freddy got over to the barn the chipmunk had gone. "He's kind of an impatient guy," Jinx said. "Fidgeted around and got cranky when you didn't show up. Said he couldn't wait all day. But he left a message for you. I don't know whether you'll want to do anything about it or not."

"I don't either, unless you tell me what it is," said Freddy.

"I *am* telling you. This chipmunk lives on Macy's farm, down on the flats. Says he's got some information about Simon and his gang."

"Simon, eh?" said Freddy thoughtfully. Old Simon was the head of a large family of thieving rats who had given the Bean animals a good deal of trouble in the past. Freddy's last fight with them had been when he had driven them out of Mr. Camphor's attic the summer before. Since then he had heard nothing of them. He shook his head. "I'm not interested in Simon. As long as he's not bothering me, I'm not going to bother him. Where's he living—over at Macy's?"

"Search me, chum," said the cat. "I'm just telling you what the guy said. You going over to see him?" When Freddy said no, Jinx said: "OK, maybe I'll gallop over there myself this afternoon. He said he wanted a dollar for his information, but I guess if I give him a touch of the old third degree he'll sing without getting paid for it. Things are kind of dull around here; I wouldn't mind a little rat hunting. So long, old kid."

Chapter 2

Mrs. Wiggins, the cow, was Freddy's partner in the detective business. Some people thought it was pretty funny for a cow to be a detective, but as a matter of fact they made a splendid team. Pigs are full of ideas, but cows are full of common sense, and when you get that combination to work on a problem it's pretty near unbeatable.

They plodded along next morning up past the duck pond and through the woods, and then across a shallow valley and up a hill, from whose top they looked down on the wide lawns of Mr. Camphor's fine estate, spread out, smooth and green, along the blue waters of the lake. They went down through the tall iron gates and up the drive to the front door.

Bannister, Mr. Camphor's butler, answered their ring. He was a tall man in a black tail coat, and he held his head so high and stiff that he couldn't see anything in front of him except his nose, which pointed right over their heads at the tops of the trees outside.

"Hello, Bannister," Freddy said. "Is Mr. Camphor expecting us?"

"Who shall I say wishes to see him?" inquired the butler.

"Mrs. Wiggins and Mr. Frederick Bean."

"Kindly step in, sir and madam," said Bannister, standing aside. "In the drawing room, please. I will announce you." And he wheeled stiffly and marched out.

"My land!" said Mrs. Wiggins crossly. "I should think we'd known Bannister long enough so he could at least say How de do."

"He isn't being snooty," said Freddy. "He's just being a good butler. He explained it to me once. A good butler has to be dignified and formal for everybody in the house. That's what he's hired for—to keep everything very high class and ceremonious. That's the advantage of having a lot of money like Mr. Camphor: if you don't want to bother about being dignified, you can hire somebody to be dignified for you."

Just then Mr. Camphor came hurriedly into the room. "Freddy!" he exclaimed. "My dear fellow! And Mrs. Wiggins! I'm so glad you've come. And not just because I need your help either. I've missed you animals; began to think all my old friends had deserted me."

"There's no friend like an old friend," put in Bannister.

Freddy grinned, remembering how Mr. Camphor and Bannister were always arguing about proverbs, and testing them out to see whether they were really true or not.

But Mr. Camphor frowned. "I think you've got that one wrong, Bannister. The one you're thinking of is 'There's no fool like an old fool,' and I fail to see where that applies to anyone in this company."

"Certainly not, sir," said Bannister, turning pink. "Forgive me, sir; I fancy I became a bit confused in the pleasure of seeing old friends."

"That's real nice of you, Bannister," said Mrs. Wiggins, "and I know you mean it. But I don't see how you can say you've seen us when you're looking over our heads all the time."

"The lady is right," Mr. Camphor said. "Relax, Bannister. As you say, we're among friends. Sit down, will you?"

"Thank you, sir," said Bannister, and sat down stiffly on the edge of a small gilt chair.

"Well, Mr. Cam—that is, Jimson," Freddy began, "we feel rather ashamed that we seem to have come only because you sent for us."

"If you hadn't come when I sent for you, you'd feel ashamed, wouldn't you? And now you say you're ashamed because you did come. I don't see how you can have it both ways, you'd just be ashamed whatever you did. Well, well; business before pleasure. Come meet Aunt Elmira."

" 'Go to the ant, thou sluggard,' " Bannister quoted.

"Eh?" said Mr. Camphor sharply. "Really, Bannister, I'd prefer you to keep your opinion of my character to yourself. Just because you're up before I am every morning . . ."

"I beg pardon, sir," said the butler. "I was not referring to you as a sluggard. That is a proverb."

"Oh, yes. Quite so. But when I mentioned my aunt, I was referring to a female relative,

not an insect. So that makes us even on referring."

"Freddy had a pet ant once," said Mrs. Wiggins. "His name was Jerry. He could read and
write."

"Very interesting," said Mr. Camphor. "But
unless we want to get hopelessly mixed up, let's
stick to the female relatives. I want you to meet
them anyway, so you'll understand why I need
your help with them."

Miss Elmira Camphor was an enormously fat
old lady who sat wrapped in shawls in a large
wheel chair out on the lawn. On her head she
wore a little old-fashioned bonnet like those
you see in the pictures of Queen Victoria, and
as they came up she peered at them through
steel-bowed spectacles with an expression of
deep gloom on her broad face.

"Aunt Elmira," said Mr. Camphor, "may I
present my friends, Mrs. Wiggins and Mr.
Frederick Bean, the celebrated poet?"

The animals bowed, and Miss Elmira didn't
say anything.

"Aunt Elmira and Aunt Minerva are spending the summer with me," Mr. Camphor explained. "They've been coming up here for
the summer for—let's see, forty years, isn't it,

Aunt? Only they've always stayed over at Lakeside. You see over there on the far shore—that big building among the trees? That's Lakeside. A summer hotel. But this year, Mrs. Filmore, who runs the place, couldn't take them. Just when she was getting ready for the summer season everything went wrong: pipes burst, porches collapsed, the help left—you never heard such a hard luck story. From what I hear, Mrs. Filmore won't even try to open the place this year. But that, you see, was my good fortune; my aunts have come to stay with me." He didn't look as if he felt very fortunate.

"It's an ill wind that blows nobody good," put in Bannister.

"Eh?" said Mr. Camphor. He looked hard at Bannister. "Well, if you call . . ." he began, and then caught himself up. "Ha, to be sure, to be sure!" he said hastily. "A delightful summer for us all," he added gloomily. "Eh, Aunt Elmira?"

Miss Elmira paid no attention to the question. She was looking at Freddy, and now her mouth opened very slowly—it was like a slow motion movie of someone speaking—and she said in a hoarse voice: "Recite!"

"She'd like you to recite one of your poems."

Freddy was puzzled. "I beg your pardon," he said; "I don't believe I . . ."

"Poem!" said Miss Elmira.

"She'd like you to recite one of your poems," Mr. Camphor explained. "Aunt Elmira is very fond of poetry."

Mrs. Wiggins always said that one of the nicest things about Freddy was that when he was asked to perform—to recite one of his poems or do card tricks—he didn't wriggle and have to be coaxed. Jinx didn't agree with her. He said: "Coaxed! You can't mention anything to that pig that doesn't remind him of some poem he's just written, and then he holds you down and reads it to you. Just a big show-off." But of course Jinx didn't like poetry much.

"There's a little thing on spring I wrote the other day," Freddy said.

> *"Spring is in the air;*
> *Birds are flying north;*
> *And though trees are bare,*
> *Now they're putting forth*
> *Leaves. The fields are green.*
> *Sun is getting higher.*
> *Monday Mr. Bean*
> *Put out the furnace fire.*
> *Birds are building nests;*
> *In the swamp are peepers;*

Men discard their vests;
Eggs are getting cheaper.
All the girls and boys—"

"Stop!" said Miss Elmira.

"I—I beg your pardon?" Freddy stammered.

"Gloomy poem," she said.

"Gloomy!" he exclaimed. "Why it's all about spring and birds singing and . . ."

"Aunt Elmira doesn't mean that your poem is gloomy," Mr. Camphor interrupted. "She wants you to *recite* a gloomy one. It's the only kind she likes."

"Oh," said Freddy. "Well, I don't believe I've ever written a gloomy one. I'm sorry, ma'am. Maybe if I get time this afternoon I could write you one."

"My aunt will be very pleased," said Mr. Camphor. "Well, if you'll excuse us, Aunt . . ." He led his guests up to the terrace on the west side of the house. "I suppose you're wondering," he said, "why I'm so anxious for your help in getting my aunts to leave."

"Well, yes," said Freddy. "Of course we've only met Miss Elmira, but I shouldn't think she'd be much bother."

"She isn't. But how'd you like to have her around all summer?"

"I guess she'd make me feel kind of depressed."

"Depressed! Ha!—just plain squashed. All day long she sits in that chair. You think of something nice to do, and then you look out the window and see her. It's as if a black cloud came over the sun. It's as if you had a stomach ache that you'd forgotten about, and then it starts up again. Nothing seems like fun, and the more you look at her, the more you wonder why you don't just go up and lock yourself in your room and set fire to the house."

"It does take the joy out of life, having her around," Freddy said. "Maybe you could get her to do something. What's she interested in?"

"Sorrow," said Mr. Camphor. "Misery. Grief, woe and tribulation."

"Well, I feel sorry for *her*," said Mrs. Wiggins. "She must have had a pretty hard life, to be so gloomy all the time."

"On the contrary," said Mr. Camphor, "she's had an easy one. Plenty of money, no troubles. Yet the more you try to cheer her up the gloomier she gets. Bannister and I have worn ourselves out trying to be pleasant, and telling jokes and so on."

"And your other aunt," said Freddy. "You said you wanted them both to leave. Is she gloomy too?"

"I'd rather you formed your own opinion," Mr. Camphor said. "I don't want you to think I'm just an old crab who can't get along with his relatives. You tell me what *you* think after you've met her. In the meantime, have you— have you any ideas?" He looked hopefully from one to the other.

"Oh, yes," said Freddy; "yes, lots of 'em. Dozens. It's only just being sure to select the right one." He spoke confidently, but although it was perfectly true that he had plenty of ideas, there wasn't a single one that was any good. It wasn't very practical, for instance, to get rid of Miss Elmira by having a giant bird, like the Roc in the Arabian Nights, fly away with her, or to tie her to a big rocket and shoot her off into space. So many of the schemes people think up for doing quite reasonable things are like that.

"Well," said Mrs. Wiggins, "I should think the sensible thing to do would be to help that Mrs. Filmore get Lakeside open for business. Your aunts would go over there then, wouldn't they?"

"My goodness," said Freddy admiringly; "why couldn't I have thought of that?"

Mrs. Wiggins laughed comfortably. "I guess you could, all right. But you're awful smart, Freddy, and you always try to think of new ways to do things. You invent new things that I couldn't think up in a month of Sundays. But if you want to get something done in a hurry, the quickest way is to work with what you've got, seems to me."

"You're right," Mr. Camphor said; "only I don't know what we can do. I've offered to help Mrs. Filmore with money. But she's proud; she won't take it, even though she's just about broke. And anyway, she says, there's more to it than that. The hotel is haunted. That's why all her help left. They were scared out."

"Haunted?" said Freddy. "Golly, I've always wanted to spend the night in a haunted house. Do you suppose there really are ghosts there?"

"Well, *I* don't suppose so for one minute," said the cow. "I don't believe in ghosts. Just the same, you won't catch me spending any nights there. I should be scairt to death."

"I don't see how you could be scared of something you don't believe in," said Mr. Camphor.

"I don't believe in driving a car seventy

miles an hour," said Bannister, "but I'd be scared to do it."

"Oh, shut up, Bannister," said Mr. Camphor, "you're trying to mix us up. Anyway, we're not going out in the car. Unless," he added, as a thought struck him, "we drive around and talk to Mrs. Filmore. Or wait a minute. It's thirty miles around the lake, and only a mile across." He looked doubtfully at Mrs. Wiggins. "I don't suppose we could all go in the canoe?"

"We'll all go in the lake if we try," said the cow. "But anyway, I'm not going. That shore over there is the southern edge of the Adirondacks—nothing but woods for miles—and woods are no place for a cow. You can't half see and you stumble over things and get twigs in your eye—and I'm not as young as I used to be. But if you two go, you ought to stay and investigate —not just talk to Mrs. Filmore. Because if you ask me, there's something funny about this ghost business. You know, Mr. Camphor, we had some trouble with a ghost once before— that old Ignormus. But he wasn't much of a ghost when you got to know him, and we nailed his hide to the barn door, didn't we, Freddy?"

"Yes, I guess we ought to look into it," said

Freddy. "But my goodness, we're detectives, not ghost busters. If we suspect somebody of something, our business is to shadow him and find out what he's up to, and if he's doing wrong, get the sheriff to put him in jail. But you can't put a ghost in a jail. And how can you shadow him?"

"Set a thief to catch a thief," said Bannister.

"Ha, you mean if you want to catch a ghost, you'd have to hire another ghost to follow him, Bannister?" said Mr. Camphor. "Not bad, not bad at all. Where can we find an unemployed ghost, Freddy? How about that Ig—Ig—"

"Ignormus," said Freddy. "He isn't around any more. Anyway, he wasn't a real ghost, and I don't believe Mrs. Filmore's is either. But I'll have to wear a disguise if I expect to find out anything. If there's somebody back of this ghost, he'll go into hiding if he sees a detective snooping around."

"Hey, I've got an idea," said Mr. Camphor. "He wouldn't suspect campers. I've got a complete camping outfit—tent, sleeping bags, everything. What do you say we go camping?"

Freddy thought it wasn't a bad idea. "But are you sure you want to go yourself? It may be dangerous."

"Danger is the spice of life," said Mr. Camphor, and Bannister said: "Faint heart ne'er won fair lady."

"Don't be silly, Bannister," Mr. Camphor said. "I don't want any fair lady; I want to have some fun. Anyway, we've got two aunts here—isn't that enough fair ladies for one summer? Well, let's look at the camping stuff."

Chapter 3

The camping outfit was certainly complete.
Mr. Camphor spread everything out on the liv-
ing-room floor, and they selected the things
they would need. There was a light-weight
eight-sided tent with a center pole, rather like
a tepee, just big enough for two people, which
Mr. Camphor said could be set up in three
minutes. There were two comfortable sleeping
bags that zipped up the sides. There was a folding table and two folding chairs, and a folding
water pail and a folding candle lantern, and

even a frying pan with a handle that folded down so that it could be packed in a bag with the cooking pails and the cups and plates and knives and spoons.

"We'll be camping in one place," Mr. Camphor said, "so we can take more stuff than we could if we had to carry it on our backs. Bannister, take one of these duffel bags and fill it up with canned goods from the storeroom. And there's a list somewhere—here it is: sugar, salt, flour; yes, fill these containers in the pantry. And we'll take this telescope, and the . . ." He stopped suddenly, and Freddy looked up and saw a tall, severe looking woman with a very long sharp nose standing in the doorway.

"Jimson Camphor!" she exclaimed in a shrill voice. "Look what you've done to this nice clean living room! All this dirty old junk strewn all over everything; why it looks like a pigpen."

"I'm sorry, Aunt Minerva," said Mr. Camphor mildly, "but you see we . . ."

"Sorry?—sorry?" she caught him up. "What good does that do? That's what you always say. Why don't you think a little beforehand? Now you clean up this mess—at once, do you hear me? And see that you wash your face and hands before lunch. I never in my life . . ." She broke off abruptly, having caught sight of Mrs. Wiggins and Freddy, and gave a sort of screech. "Oh! Animals! Animals in the living room! Jimson, have you gone stark, staring crazy?"

"Why, these are friends of mine, Aunt Minerva," he said, and tried to introduce them. But she wouldn't listen. "Get them out of here!" she demanded. "Shoo!" she said to Mrs. Wiggins, making shooing motions with her hands. "Outside! Scat!"

Freddy and Mrs. Wiggins looked at each other, and the cow's left eyelid drooped over a large brown eye. Then they started for the door.

"Animals!" Miss Minerva exclaimed disgustedly. "Animals in the house!"

"Well, what's the matter with that?" said Mr. Camphor. He was very red in the face, but he spoke calmly. "After all, you and I are animals too, Aunt Minerva."

"Oh, are we!" said his aunt sarcastically. "Are we indeed! And I suppose that is why you wish to turn this house into a stable. How dare you call me an animal!"

"All right, all right," said Mr. Camphor wearily. "We'll go out." He picked up the sleeping bags. "Freddy, take the tent. Bannister'll bring the rest."

Out on the lawn they could still hear Miss Minerva scolding and complaining. Mr. Camphor looked shamefacedly at his friends. "I'm sorry," he said. "I know I ought to have stood up for you better. After all, it *is* my house."

Freddy grinned. "Not any more, it isn't."

"I guess you're right, at that." Mr. Camphor sighed. "It's been like this ever since she got here. She drove my cook away the third day. Does the cooking herself now. But she's not much good. Burns everything. I don't suppose she burns *everything*, really. But you know how it is; after a while everything *tastes* burned."

"I'm kind of burned up myself," said Freddy.

"I know. I'm sorry about that remark she made about the pigpen . . ."

"Oh, forget it," Freddy said. "I didn't mean that. It's for you I'm burned up. A gloomy aunt outside and a cranky aunt inside; there isn't much peace and quiet for you anywhere. Unless you just move right out."

"And if I did," Mr. Camphor said, "she'd go right along with me. She says I don't know the first thing about running a house, and it's a blessing she came to stay when she did, because the place is going to rack and ruin the way I run it. She says it's her duty to look after me. You see, I was an orphan, and she brought me up. I went to live with my aunts when I was five, and the trouble was, as I got older, Aunt Minerva always treated me as if I was still the same age. Now that I'm forty she still does."

"And maybe you'll excuse my saying so," put in Mrs. Wiggins, "but with her, you still act as if you were five years old yourself."

"What do you mean?" Mr. Camphor asked, and then answered his own question. "Oh, I know; she orders me around, and I obey her and don't answer back. But after all, she's my aunt. And then, she's my guest, too. You have to be polite to guests."

"Land sakes, up to a certain point you do," said Mrs. Wiggins. "But when the guest has such bad manners that she yells at you and orders you out of your own home, she isn't a guest any more. And doing what she tells you is all right too, when you're five, or even when you're twenty. But good grief, when you're a grown-up man . . ." She stopped. "I'm talking too much," she said.

"On the contrary," said Mr. Camphor.

"You're perfectly right. I shouldn't give in to her. But I do hate unpleasantness."

"You get it anyway," said the cow.

Mr. Camphor frowned. "Everything's very difficult. Here I've asked you to come up and stay a few days and now I've got to take my invitation back. You see how she acts. I can't even have you stay to lunch. Not that it would be any treat, everything tasting burned."

"I still don't see why you let her get away with it," said Mrs. Wiggins.

"Why, because I didn't want to get her mad."

"But she couldn't *get* mad; she was mad anyway."

"H'm," said Mr. Camphor, "that's an idea. She's mad anyway; I get the unpleasantness anyway; so why shouldn't I do what I want to, eh?"

"She can get madder," said Bannister.

"I doubt it. If she did, she'd just burst."

"And what a break that would be!" said the butler.

"Come, Bannister—no slang," said Mr. Camphor. "Well, we'll try it. Two extra places for lunch, Bannister. Though I don't know," he said doubtfully; "it won't be very pleasant for you two."

"We won't mind, if it'll help you out," Freddy said. "I suppose she doesn't—she won't throw things at us?"

"Frankly, I don't know. Except for bad temper and a good deal of yelling, she's always been a lady. I don't think she'll throw anything —not anything very big, anyway. But you'd better be ready to duck."

They took the camping things down and stowed them in the canoe, and then went back to the house. When Bannister announced lunch, they went into the dining room. Miss Minerva was still in the kitchen. Mrs. Wiggins was seated at Mr. Camphor's right, and Freddy opposite her. Freddy, of course, could handle his knife, fork and spoon with ease, and even with elegance, but cows seldom acquire such skills, and indeed would find but little use for them, and so when Bannister brought in the soup plates, he put before Mrs. Wiggins a large platter of freshly cut alfalfa. Which was certainly very thoughtful of him.

It was then that Miss Minerva came in. She had been standing over the stove, and her glasses were a little fogged with the steam from the cooking, so that when Freddy rose politely and pulled out her chair she merely

He put before Mrs. Wiggins a large platter of freshly cut alfalfa.

said "Thank you" rather ungraciously, and sat down and began to eat. Then as her glasses cleared she raised her eyes—and with a loud angry cry she jumped up, so violently that her chair crashed over backward on the floor. "Jimson!" she exclaimed furiously. "What are these —these creatures doing here? Now, clear them out! I spoke to you once about them and I shan't speak to you again."

Mr. Camphor squinched his eyes up and seemed to be trying to lift his shoulders to cover his ears, but Freddy gave him a poke under the table and whispered: "Come on; we're right with you." So he straightened his shoulders and looked up and said quietly: "Oh, I think you will, Aunt."

"What's that?" she snapped. "Such impertinence! How dare you speak to me like that? Bringing these disgusting animals to the lunch table, and then saying you think I will!"

"Will what, Aunt Minerva?" he asked.

"Will—will . . ." She got mixed up and sputtered for a minute like a pinwheel, going round and round and throwing off sparks, but not getting anywhere in particular. Then as Freddy and Mr. Camphor continued to eat their soup, and Mrs. Wiggins to munch her alfalfa, she drew a deep breath and said: "Very well! Very well! If you choose to bring the farmyard into your dining room, I wash my hands of you. I've never eaten with pigs, and I'm not going to begin at my age."

"Better late than never, eh, Bannister?" said Mr. Camphor, and giggled faintly into his soup spoon.

"As you say, sir," the butler replied. "There's no time like the present."

Miss Minerva turned and stamped out of the room. But before Freddy could congratulate his host on his success, she came back and sat down determinedly in her chair. "I'm not going to be driven out of my own home by a parcel of animals, even if you haven't the decency to drive them out," she said. Then she turned to Mrs. Wiggins. "I should think you'd be ashamed to force yourself in here where you're not wanted," she said.

"Well, ma'am," said the cow, "if that's what you think, that's what you think," and went on eating.

Miss Minerva started on her soup. She didn't say anything more for a while, but kept glancing with distaste at Freddy, and then putting her handkerchief to her nose and turning away.

And at last this made Mr. Camphor angry. He could stand her picking on him, but he wasn't going to have her picking on his friends. He said: "Does the soup smell burned to you, Aunt?"

"The soup is excellent," she snapped, "and much too good for the company." And she glanced at Freddy and put her handkerchief up again.

Mr. Camphor drew himself up. Although he hired Bannister to be dignified for him, he could be pretty dignified himself when he had to. "Then if you can't be polite to my guests," he said, "you had better leave the table."

She dropped her spoon and looked at him as if she couldn't believe her ears. "*You* are telling *me* to leave the table!" she exclaimed. "How dare you, Jimson Camphor!" She glared at him, but he returned the look sternly, and in a minute she dropped her eyes. She picked up her soup spoon and said in a quieter voice: "That I should live to see the day when you would insult me like this! This I can never forgive." Then, as he didn't say any more, she went on eating. But she didn't put her handkerchief to her nose again.

After a time Freddy said: "Very good soup, Jimson. Delicious."

It was really terrible soup, and badly burned into the bargain. Mr. Camphor said shortly: "H'mp, glad you like it." But Miss Minerva turned and looked for the first time full at Freddy. "The first word of praise for my cooking that I've ever heard in this house," she said; "and it had to come from a pig!" But nobody answered her, and for the rest of the meal she was silent.

Bannister took out the soup plates and brought in an omelet—which was scorched— and, for Mrs. Wiggins, a big bowl of hay, with a side dish of oats. The dessert, an Indian pudding, was also burned, but the sauce was good, and they ate that. Mrs. Wiggins, however, ate her pudding and all of Freddy's. She smacked her lips rather too loud over it, but Miss Minerva didn't seem to be offended, and even gave her a vinegary smile.

After lunch, when Miss Minerva had gone back to the kitchen, they sat for a while on the terrace.

"You know, Freddy," Mr. Camphor said, "this is the first meal I've sat through with

Aunt Minerva that she hasn't scolded me from the time she unfolded her napkin to the time she pushed back her chair. I believe maybe you and Mrs. Wiggins have shown me how to get along with her."

"You mean praising the food?" Freddy asked.

"No, I mean going ahead and doing what I want to in my own house."

"Well, good land, it wouldn't hurt you to pay her a little compliment now and then," said the cow. "If you praised her cooking she might improve it."

"Maybe. But even if she did, she'd still object to everything I do. Anyway, I couldn't. If I'd tried to compliment her on that awful soup, the words would have stuck halfway out. How you ever ate that pudding, Mrs. Wiggins . . ."

"I liked it."

"Well, there's no accounting for tastes," said Mr. Camphor, and Bannister, who was taking a luncheon tray down to Miss Elmira, said: "The proof of the pudding is in the eating."

"Who wants to eat the terrible stuff?" said Mr. Camphor. "No, you see," he went on, "I've always done what she wanted me to, even the silliest things, just to save trouble. But it didn't save anything—I got yelled at just the same. Yes, after this I'm going to . . ."

"Jimson!" came Miss Minerva's voice from the kitchen window. "Don't sit out on that damp terrace without your rubbers. Go get them on at once!"

Mr. Camphor got up. "Yes, Aunt Minerva . . ." He stopped short. Freddy and Mrs. Wiggins were frowning ferociously at him. He sat down again.

"Hurry up, Jimson," Miss Minerva shouted. "I'm not going to nurse you through another of your colds."

Mr. Camphor waved a hand airily at her, then turned away and began talking to the animals. Miss Minerva glared for a minute, then slammed the window down hard.

Chapter 4

News travels fast in the forest. By sundown every deer and fox and coon, every squirrel and chipmunk within a radius of twenty miles knew that Mr. C. Jimson Camphor and a friend from the city were camping on Jones's Bay, quarter of a mile below Lakeside. What they did not know, of course, was that the friend from the city was Freddy. They supposed him to be a Dr. Henry Hopper.

Freddy had realized that his identity must be carefully concealed. He knew that the minute they pulled the canoe up on the shore dozens of curious eyes would be watching every move, and dozens of sharp ears listening to every word. And once the woods animals learned that the famous pig detective was camping beside the lake, it wouldn't be long before the whole countryside knew it too.

Fortunately Mr. Camphor had a lot of old camping clothes packed away in mothballs, and from these Freddy picked out a lumberman's flannel shirt in big black and red checks, a pair of blue work pants, some red and white striped woolen socks, and some high-laced boots, which though too large for his trotters, worked fairly well when he stuffed an extra pair of socks into them before putting them on. He had decided not to wear false whiskers, as they were sure to be troublesome when walking through brush. But in order to conceal his face as much as possible, he selected an old-fashioned coonskin cap that had belonged to Mr. Camphor's grandfather, who had been a well-known trapper. It was pretty hot, but it came well down over his eyes and had a tail that hung down behind. In this outfit, Freddy was just such a small perspiring camper as you might meet on any Adirondack trail. Even the strong smell of mothballs was right in character.

Among the camping things was a small leather case, like a doctor's case, containing a first aid kit and a few simple remedies, which Mr. Camphor said his aunt had made him buy to take on his first camping trip. On the side was the manufacturer's name: Henry Hopper & Co. He scraped off the "& Co." and lettered "M.D." in its place with ink. "I don't know why I never thought of disguising myself as a doctor before," said Freddy. "With a doctor's case in my hand I could get in anywhere."

Along the north shore of the lake, the woods came right down to the water, but on the east side of Jones's Bay was Stony Point, and beside the point a short stretch of sandy beach. At the edge of this Mr. Camphor pitched the tent. He picked out a level spot, cleared off the brush with his hatchet and pounded down one or two hummocks to make it smooth, then unrolled and spread out the tent, pegged down the eight corners, and going inside, set up the center pole. The whole thing took less than ten minutes.

In another half hour they had unpacked the canoe, set up the table and chairs in front of the tent, and when Mr. Camphor had built a little fireplace of two rows of flat stones, set about four inches apart, he filled a pail with water for the tea, and began mixing batter for flapjacks.

"Hadn't I better start the fire?" said Freddy.

"You've never camped before, have you?" said Mr. Camphor. "Well . . . go ahead if you want to."

So Freddy gathered a few handfuls of twigs and lit them between the stones. They were dry and flared up nicely. They flared up so nicely that in two minutes they were almost gone and Freddy had to forage for more. This happened several times, and each time Freddy had to go farther and take longer to get another supply. And the last time the fire went out before he could get back.

"Oh, dear," he said, "I guess I ought to have collected plenty of wood first, hadn't I?"

"Can you use a hatchet?" said Mr. Camphor. "There are some black birch saplings back of the tent. Cut three or four of the small ones and drag them around here. They'll burn green. Get plenty of twigs and sticks going, and then put your birch on. It'll burn down to coals, and we need coals to cook the flapjacks." He put down the bowl of batter and opened a package of bacon. "There's no point in camping if you're going to be uncomfortable," he said.

enough

"And the secret of being comfortable is never doing anything until you are prepared. Never put up your tent until you've made the ground level. Never light your fire till you have gathered all the fuel you'll need." He got out the plates and knives and forks and began to set the table.

Freddy's second fire was more successful. He made it too large, as most beginners do. A tiny flame will heat a pail of water in a few minutes, and a few handfuls of coals will fry all the flapjacks a man and a pig can eat. They had butter and maple syrup on their flapjacks, and took turns cooking them. Mr. Camphor showed Freddy how to flip them. He was an expert. When a flapjack was done on one side, he would give the frying pan a flip, and the flapjack would go up and make three complete turns in the air before landing back squarely in the pan, uncooked side down. Freddy's first one flew up into a tree and stayed there; his second was a success, though a sloppy one, for it hit the edge of the pan and half of it went into the fire. After that he did better. It was so much fun flipping them that he ate sixteen.

After the sixteenth Freddy groaned and

Freddy's first one flew up into a tree.

stretched out lazily in his chair. "Ho! Whee!" he said. "This is the life!"

"Ho, whee yourself," said Mr. Camphor. "If you're through, you can wash the dishes."

"What—*now?*" said Freddy.

"No good camper ever leaves dirty dishes around," said Mr. Camphor, and handed him the frying pan.

Freddy went into the tent and rummaged in the pack. "Where's the dishpan?" he called.

Mr. Camphor called him back. "There's your dishpan, my boy," he said, pointing to the lake. "A bunch of grass for a dishrag, and a handful of sand for soap, and you'll be surprised how clean you can scour things."

After everything was washed and put away, Mr. Camphor got out the telescope and set it up on a tripod and peered through it across the lake. "Let's see what's going on at home," he said. "Ha, there's Bannister coming down to wheel Aunt Elmira into the house. Want to look?"

Freddy put his eye to the glass. The distant shore seemed to leap up to within a few yards. There was Miss Elmira sitting in her chair, so close that he could have seen the expression on her face if there had been any. Which of course there wasn't. Bannister stood in front of her; as Freddy watched, he went around behind the chair and started to wheel it towards the house. "Goodness!" said Freddy. For the butler had bent down and made a hideous face at the old lady's back.

"What is it?" said Mr. Camphor, and as Freddy moved aside and let him look: "Gracious me!" he said. "I didn't know Bannister felt as strongly about her as that!" And after a minute: "Why, he's remarkably talented! Ha, I wonder if I could do that one. How's this, Freddy?" He turned towards the pig and wrinkled up his nose and sort of pulled all his other features close up around it.

"Not bad," said Freddy. "But look." He rolled his eyes up, stretched his mouth wide, and then twisted his snout to one side.

"Heavens!" said Mr. Camphor. "Stop it, Freddy; that's too awful! Why, you don't even look human. Ha, well; of course you don't anyway, but I mean, couldn't you injure your face doing that?"

"We used to play a game," Freddy said; "sit around and make faces, and the most horrible one got a prize."

"You must show me your prizes some time,"

Mr. Camphor said. "I'll bet you've got a roomful." He glanced at the sun which was just touching the western hills. "Let's build up the fire; it will be chilly when the sun sets. We'll drag some of those dead branches down. Don't bother to chop them up; we'll put the butts in the fire and move them up as they burn. Oh, not that piece, Freddy; it's hemlock; snaps and throws sparks all over the place."

"Pssst!" Freddy whispered, for he had heard the rustle of some small animal in the underbrush. "Not so loud with the name; remember who I am."

"Sorry," muttered Mr. Camphor. He sat down on a log and poked at the fire with a stick. "Well, Dr. Hopper," he said in a loud voice, "you were going to tell me some of your experiences in the wilds of Africa, were you not?"

"So I was, Mr. Camphor, sir; so I was," said Freddy pompously. "Well, sir, as you know, my purpose in going to Africa was to study the methods of the native witch doctors in curing disease. These methods are rather different from the regular American medical practice, and include putting on false faces, dancing around the patient, and banging on drums and yelling. All this looks pretty silly to doctors who just give pills and look at your tongue. But the odd thing is that the patients often get well.

"Successful as this treatment is, only a few American doctors use it. You can see why. If you, sir, came down with the flu, and your doctor, instead of taking your temperature and looking very solemn, were to dress up in a leopard skin and a clown mask and dance around your bed screeching and shaking a rattle, you might be sort of irritated."

It was getting dark. Freddy glanced around. Here and there in the underbrush sparks glowed steadily in pairs—the eyes of small animals reflecting the firelight. It was the audience that always surrounds a campfire at night.

"However," Freddy went on, "from medical treatment I was led into the study of magic, which the witch doctors go in for a lot."

"Ha, magic!" said Mr. Camphor. "I have a friend who is a magician—Freddy. You may have heard of him."

"I have attended his performances," Freddy replied. "A remarkably clever pig. However, as I was saying, I studied magic. I studied under M'glumpas, the most celebrated witch doctor in Africa. I became expert in the weaving of spells and the manufacture of wishing caps—

you know, you put them on and then wish for whatever you want."

"And do you get your wish?"

"Sometimes. And sometimes not. All depending."

"On what?"

"Oh, on general conditions. This and that."

"Very clear," said Mr. Camphor. "From your description I feel that I could almost make one myself. But continue."

"Later," said Freddy, "I learned to work transformations. Take a man, for instance, and change him into a—well, into a pig. That's where I got into trouble. I was practicing one day, and I changed old M'glimpy into a tree . . ."

"Thought his name was M'glumpas," said Mr. Camphor.

"M'glimpy was his first name. Full name: M'glimpy M'glumpas. Anyhow, there he was, a hundred-foot bongo tree, and I had forgotten how to change him back again. And of course he couldn't tell me; he could just rustle. Boy, how he rustled! He was pretty mad. I left Africa in a hurry. Good thing I hadn't changed him into an elephant or a crocodile, wasn't it?"

"What's that?" Mr. Camphor exclaimed. He

jumped up and listened. "It sounded like a shot."

Freddy had heard it too, but only faintly, because the coonskin cap was so tight over his ears. "Must be a long way off," he said.

"I don't think so," Mr. Camphor said. "Sounds don't travel very far in the woods. It came from the direction of Lakeside. Let's go down and look; there's a trail along the shore."

Chapter 5

Freddy and Mr. Camphor stumbled along the trail by the light of their candle lantern, and pretty soon through the trees they saw a faint yellow glow. Then they came out in a clearing, and beyond them was the dark bulk of the hotel, with a light in one of the downstairs windows. Something moved on the porch, and a woman's voice said: "Stop right where you are!"

"It's me, Mrs. Filmore," said Mr. Camphor.

"We're camping down by the point, and we thought we heard a shot."

"You did. Come in and I'll tell you about it."

They went up on the porch and followed her through the darkened lounge into a small office, lit by a kerosene lamp. She was a tall nice-looking woman with a worried expression on her face and a pistol in her hand. She put the pistol in a desk drawer, but she kept the worried expression on, and said: "I'm glad to see somebody human, though—" she smiled—"you do smell dreadfully of mothballs. There are things going on here . . . well, I've never been much of a believer in ghosts, but it's got so now, with the rapping and groaning and footsteps in empty rooms and wild Indians peering in through windows that nobody can get a wink of sleep all night."

"Let me present my friend, Dr. Hopper," said Mr. Camphor. "He's rather an authority on ghosts; perhaps he can help you."

"Too late for that," said Mrs. Filmore. "I've given up. I'm leaving tonight." She pointed to several suitcases which stood by the door.

"I'm sorry to hear that," Mr. Camphor said.

"I'm going to drive to Centerboro, going to

stay with my cousin, Mrs. Lafayette Bingle for a while. Until I can find a job."

"I know Mrs. Bingle," said Freddy, forgetting for a moment that he was Dr. Hopper. "Please remember me to her. I—I attended her professionally."

This was quite true, but it had been as a detective in a matter of lost spectacles, not as a doctor.

"If your going is a question of money," Mr. Camphor began.

She shook her head. "You're very kind. It's true of course, I have no more money to pay workmen. But even if I felt that I could accept a loan, I doubt if all the money in the world could get this place in shape to open. As soon as one thing is fixed another breaks down. And my help has all left. No, I shall have to sell for what I can get. There!" she said, as there came a series of loud knocks from somewhere upstairs. "How long do you think a waitress or a handy man would stay with that kind of thing going on? And if the help stayed, how would my guests like it? No," she said as Mr. Camphor reached for his lantern, "there's no use going to look; there won't be anybody there."

"Well, ma'am," said Freddy, "don't you

think somebody real is behind all this? I mean, some enemy? Who could come up every night and put on a ghost show?"

"How would they come?" she asked. "How could they get here—in a car, a motor boat—without my hearing them?" She looked at him curiously, her eyes disapproving of the coonskin cap, which of course he had had to keep on to avoid being recognized as a pig.

"I hope you'll excuse my wearing my cap," he said. "You see, I . . ." Then he stopped. He couldn't think of any reason why Dr. Hopper couldn't take the cap off.

But Mrs. Filmore was too upset to care. "I've given up guessing what it's all about," she said. She pointed to the window, in which there was a small round hole. "That was the shot you heard. There was a face, and I fired at it. I couldn't have missed. But when I went outside there was nothing there." She got up. "You'll excuse me, but it's getting late and I must go."

They helped her carry the bags out to the car. As they watched the red tail-light bobbing and jigging over the rough narrow track that followed the shore three miles out to the state road, Mr. Camphor sighed. "I don't know what the poor woman's going to live on. Every cent she had was in this hotel. A haunted hotel! My goodness, what could you do with that?"

"I bet she could get a lot of people to come and stay," said Freddy. "People who want to show off how brave they are."

"Not if she couldn't get cooks and waitresses to stay. I guess I'm brave enough to meet a ghost, but I'm not brave enough to stay at a hotel where they don't serve meals."

"No, I guess I'm not either. You know what Napoleon said: an army travels on its stomach."

"On its stomach!" Mr. Camphor exclaimed. "Ha, I'd like to see an army do that. It couldn't make a mile a day."

"I think he meant that an army can't be brave unless it has plenty to eat," Freddy said.

"Well, why didn't he say so then? That's a pretty roundabout way of saying something that everybody knows anyway." He turned quickly to Freddy. "Look," he said, "we've had plenty to eat. We're so full of flapjacks that our arms and legs stick right out straight like those little rubber balloon men that you blow up. We ought to be brave enough to tackle a haunted house. What do you say we spend the night here? Maybe we could find out something about this ghost, eh?"

"Why, sure, sure," Freddy said. "Only—well, had we ought to leave all our stuff unprotected?"

"Who's going to run off with it—the squirrels and the chipmunks?"

"No, but we're supposed to be camping—roughing it, sort of. Isn't it kind of sissy to spend the very first night you're out camping in a hotel?"

"H'm," said Mr. Camphor, "well now you mention it I guess you're right. Anyway, we can see better to explore the place by daylight." He turned to lead the way back along the trail, and then swung round suddenly. "No!" he said determinedly. "We're just kidding ourselves. We're afraid—we're scared of all those empty rooms, and the darkness and the noises. Well anyway, I am."

Freddy glanced at the black bulk of the hotel and thought of those heavy knocks, and of faces looking in the windows—ferocious Indian faces—and shivered. "Oh, dear," he said; "I remember saying to somebody, or was it somebody said it to me?—anyway it was when that Ignormus had us all so scared, and I said, or somebody said, if you were scared of something you ought to walk right up to it and say Boo! And then you'd find there wasn't anything to be scared of at all." He shivered again. "It—it seemed a good idea at the time."

"I don't think saying Boo is such a good idea," Mr. Camphor said. "I mean, what would it get you? I mean, a ghost—wouldn't he think you were kind of silly if you just stood there and said Boo?—Oh, come on, Fred—I mean, Doctor. We're going to feel pretty cheap tomorrow morning if we just go back to the camp now."

So Freddy said unhappily: "All right," and they went back into the hotel. In the office they relit the oil lamp, then brought two long cushioned wicker settees in from the lounge, and, turning the light down a little, had just settled comfortably on them when . . .

Tap, tap, tap, tap. Somebody was rapping on the window.

Freddy shut his eyes tight and pretended not to hear anything.

Tap, tap, tap! Slower and louder. Freddy felt a procession of ants with very cold feet walking up his backbone.

"D—did you hear something?" Mr. Camphor whispered.

Freddy gave a gentle snore.

"Oh, come on," said Mr. Camphor. "You can't be asleep yet. Look, you're facing that window—I can't see it without turning around, and I—I might scare 'em. Just take a peek, will you?"

But Freddy wasn't taking any peeks. He didn't see how he could be any more scared than he was, but he knew if he saw what was at the window he would be. He squeezed his eyelids so tight together that he saw stars and pinwheels.

Rap, rap, *crash*! Something had smashed the window, and as the bits of glass tinkled on the floor, Freddy and Mr. Camphor jumped up and grabbed each other. Looking through the jagged hole in the glass was the head of a huge cat. It was as big as a man's head and it had fierce whiskers. It stared ferociously at them and then dropped out of sight.

They hung on to each other for a minute, then Mr. Camphor let go and ran over and pulled down the windowshade while Freddy turned up the lamp.

Mr. Camphor's teeth still chattered a little as he said reproachfully: "You hadn't ought to have tried to get behind me, Freddy."

"Get behind you!" Freddy exclaimed. "It was you that was trying to get behind *me*!"

"Oh, well," said Mr. Camphor, "I guess we

were both trying to get behind each other. And that would be kind of hard, wouldn't it? We might try it again sometime when we aren't busy. I guess . . ." He stopped short and grabbed Freddy's shoulder. "Look!" For the door into the darkened lounge, which they had pulled shut, was opening very, very slowly.

And as it opened they backed, just as slowly, away from it. They backed, without thinking of it, right up against the window. And when their shoulders touched the drawn shade, from outside, almost in their ears, came a long wailing screech.

That finished them. They both jumped a foot in the air, and when they came down they were running. They jammed together for a moment in the doorway, and the next thing they knew, they were half way down the trail to Stony Point. They only stopped then because Mr. Camphor tripped over a root and fell, and Freddy stumbled over him.

They lay panting where they had fallen. "Lucky—didn't break our necks," Mr. Camphor wheezed. For they had of course left their lantern in the hotel, and though the night was clear, there was no moon, and the starshine was

It was as big as a man's head and it had fierce whiskers.

too faint to be of any use to eyes that had just left a lighted room.

Gradually their eyes became accustomed to the darkness and they got up and went on. Their campfire had burned down, but the embers still glowed, and when they threw on fresh wood the flames leaped up and the light flickered on the green leaves and brown tree trunks that surrounded them, on the bottom of the overturned canoe and on the . . . "Where on earth is the tent?" Freddy said suddenly.

They ran over to it. It was there, but it was a complete wreck. The loops by which it was pegged to the ground were cut so that the center pole had fallen over, there were long slits in the canvas, and all their supplies were scattered about outside. Everything that could be torn was torn, and everything that could be spilt was spilt.

"The canoe, Freddy!" Mr. Camphor exclaimed, and they hurried down to the beach. But the canoe hadn't been touched.

"You know, that's funny," he said. "They smashed everything else; why leave the canoe?"

"Maybe it's kind of a hint that they want us to get in it and go," said Freddy.

"Maybe so. But smashing our stuff would be

hint enough, wouldn't it? My goodness, I'm glad they just hinted and didn't say right out what they meant." He went back and began poking around in the wreckage. "Well, here's the frying pan and the pail. The canned stuff is all right. And we've got a hatchet. Why Freddy, with these and our sleeping bags we've still got a camping outfit. You know, maybe I'm the kind of person that can't take a hint, because I don't think I'm going back home— I'm going right on with this camping trip. We'll paddle across tomorrow and get some guns, so if these people give us any more hints, we can hint right back at them. How about it?"

Freddy said: "It wasn't any ghost that wrecked the camp, and I want to look it over by daylight. Maybe there'll be some clues. Sure, I'll stick. But where will we sleep?"

"In the sleeping bags. They're not entirely ruined. And I guess it will be a pretty tough mosquito that'll try to get through this smell of mothballs to bite us.

"But it might rain. We'd better build a lean-to shelter. Let's see, we want about three ten-foot poles and some shorter ones. We can roof it with what's left of the tent. Let's have the hatchet."

Chapter 6

Mr. Camphor had been right: they slept peacefully. The mosquitoes came singing through the trees, gave one sniff, and then flew off, whining angrily, in search of more savory game. The ghost didn't bother them either. And when they woke up in the morning, and the sun was slanting through the trees and sparkling on the lake, they felt a lot more cheerful.

Only there wasn't anything for breakfast.

"Why can't we paddle across and have breakfast at your house?" said Freddy.

"With Aunt Minerva?" Mr. Camphor inquired.

"H'm," said Freddy. "Burnt toast. Let's see if there aren't some supplies in the hotel."

They washed in the lake—Freddy had to keep his coonskin cap on for fear of being recognized by the woods animals, but he got the lower part of his face clean—and then took the trail to Lakeside. Mr. Camphor went out to the kitchen, but Freddy said he wanted to go into the office to look for clues.

He found one almost at once. A long piece of cord was tied to the outside knob of the door that opened into the lounge. "So that was the way our ghost made the door open so slowly," he said to himself.

In the office he looked in the desk drawer for Mrs. Filmore's pistol, but it was gone. "The ghost came back after we left," he thought. "Probably wanted to get that gun. That's why he opened that door and then ran around outside and yelled at the window so we'd clear out."

Pretty soon Mr. Camphor came back from the kitchen. "Nothing there," he said. "But I found half a loaf of bread and a glass of currant jelly."

Freddy showed him the cord.

"Our ghost, eh?" he said. "How disappointing! Dear me, I'd almost begun to believe in him."

Freddy said: "I should think you'd be glad to find out that whoever is causing all this trouble is real flesh and blood."

"Well, I'm not. I'd much rather have a ghost to fight. What can a ghost do?"

"He can scare you half to death."

"And that's all he can do," said Mr. Camphor. "He can't sneak up and hit you with a club. All he can do is yell in your ear. I bet you if a ghost jumped out and yelled at you, and you just laughed at him, he'd burst into tears. My goodness, I feel kind of sorry for ghosts; they can't do a thing but glide around in sheets and moan and make scary noises. I suppose that's why they don't ever seem to accomplish much."

"Well, you can have your ghosts," Freddy said. "I'd rather be hit with a club than scared into fits. And how about that giant cat that looked in the window—was that real?"

"Oh, it was real all right. I never saw a cat that big, but it might be some kind of leopard.

I've heard of people training them to hunt. If it was . . ." He shivered.

"It was a man in a false face," said Freddy. "Oh, yes it was! Because I saw its eyes move, and they were brown. I've seen cats with yellow eyes, and with green, and even blue ones, but I never yet saw a cat with brown eyes."

"You know what I think?" said Mr. Camphor after a minute. "That man, whoever he is, is trying to scare people away from this hotel. He's been pretty successful at it, so he'll keep on playing ghost. And that means that he won't show himself in the daytime. So today is our chance to look around and try to find out something about him."

They ate their bread and jelly and then went to work. "You know," said Mr. Camphor, "what puzzles me is how the ghost gets up here. And where does he go in the daytime? He can't just live in the woods; he must come nights. I checked the tire marks out in the road—the only ones are Mrs. Filmore's."

"I guess he glides," Freddy said. "You know —just comes kind of floating through the trees with a kind of faint fizzing noise."

"Let's have a look at the cellar," said Mr.

Camphor. "You can tell more about folks by looking around their cellar than anywhere else in the house."

The cellar was a mess. A water pipe had burst and flooded it and evidently Mrs. Filmore hadn't been able to get the break repaired. She had just turned the water off. Freddy examined the pipe, then he said: "Look here—this pipe didn't break; it was gnawed."

"Oh, go on," said Mr. Camphor. "I don't believe even an alligator could gnaw through an iron pipe."

"I don't suppose one ever tried," Freddy said. "Anyway, this pipe isn't iron,—it's lead. And look at the teeth marks. My guess is if we look again at those beams that fell down under the porch, we'll find the same marks." He looked meaningly at his friend. "And do you know who made them?"

"Don't look at me," Mr. Camphor protested. "I didn't do it."

"No ghost has strong enough teeth to do it either," said Freddy. "Rats did it. And I'm afraid I know their names."

"You don't mean those rats that were in my attic last year?"

"Simon and his gang—yes. After we drove

them out of your house they could have got around the lake and up here, I suppose. This is just the kind of place they like—a big rambling building with a storeroom full of food. Let's look at the pantry."

But there was no sign of rats in the pantry, nor could they find any rat holes anywhere in the hotel.

"That's queer," Freddy said. "I'm sure it was rats that tore up those hotel bedrooms, and it was rats that wrecked our camp: those tent loops were gnawed, not cut. It's the kind of vandalism rats think is fun. But I never knew 'em to pass up a good feed, and that pantry must have been full of supplies."

"Speaking of supplies," said Mr. Camphor, "I'd better paddle over and get some."

Freddy said maybe he'd better go—he wanted to get Mrs. Wiggins' advice.

"All right," said Mr. Camphor. "Can you manage a canoe?"

Until Mr. Camphor had paddled him across the lake yesterday, Freddy had never been in a canoe. But it had looked pretty easy. "Oh, sure," he said confidently. So they went back to camp, and Freddy turned the canoe over and slid it into the water and got in.

Now when he sat down in the stern seat, his weight made the bow come right up out of the water. He took a stroke with the paddle as he had seen Mr. Camphor do. But instead of going ahead, the canoe swung halfway around, and a second stroke whirled it farther, so that it was now pointing back to the shore.

"You'll have to put a rock in the bow to keep it down," Mr. Camphor called. "You won't be able to manage it at all when you get out where there's a breeze."

Freddy could see that this made sense, but how was he to get a rock? He was ten yards from shore. He tried two more strokes, and then he was twenty yards from shore, and had made one more complete revolution.

"The blame thing keeps skidding!" he shouted. "How do you make it go straight?"

Mr. Camphor shouted back some instructions, but the breeze had caught the canoe now and blown it still farther out, and Freddy couldn't understand the words. He paddled furiously, and the harder he paddled the faster he whirled, and every time he came around he saw Mr. Camphor standing on the shore, yelling and waving his arms, and growing smaller and smaller in the distance.

His weight made the bow come right up out of the water.

It was a good thing for Freddy that the breeze was blowing in the direction he wanted to go, or goodness knows where he would have ended up. As it was, he was blown right across the lake and landed not far from Mr. Camphor's house. Bannister, who had been watching, came down and helped pull the canoe up, and told him that Mrs. Wiggins had gone back home.

"I'll have to go down, too," said Freddy. "There are some things I have to see to at the farm. Here's a list of things Mr. Camphor made out; if you'll get them ready I'll be back this afternoon and . . . Golly, how'll I get across the lake?"

But Bannister said he could paddle him over, so when Freddy had taken off his camping disguise—which wasn't necessary on this side of the lake—he started for the Bean farm.

Mrs. Wiggins had told the animals all about Lakeside, and about Mr. Camphor's aunts, and they crowded around Freddy, firing questions, and suggesting plans for getting rid of Miss Elmira and Miss Minerva.

"Quiet! Quiet!" he said. "I can't hear myself think. Now listen, animals. Mrs. Wiggins has told you that our friend Mr. Camphor is in need of help. But the case is more serious than we thought. It's a question of getting rid, not only of aunts, but of a gang of . . . I don't know what to call them, because I don't know just what they are up to. But I can tell you who I think one of them is: our old friend, Simon."

The animals exclaimed. "Simon! That scaly-tailed old sneak! Let's go up and lick 'em; we did it once!"

Charles, the rooster, flew up on a fence post. "Ladies and gentlemen," he cried. "Comrades on many a hard-fought field! You have heard the glorious news. Again our ancient enemy raises his foul head; again, the leader of a cruel and vindictive horde of savage barbarians, he menaces the peace that like a soft blanket broods over the hills of Bean. Rise, animals, in your might; let the old battle cry resound: Claws and teeth, comrades; claws and teeth!— Ouch!" he yelled suddenly, as his wife, Henri-etta, seized him by the tailfeathers and pulled him down.

"You and your brooding blanket!" she said sarcastically. "You and your foul head! Now you rise in your might and go on back to the henhouse, so we can hear what Freddy has to say."

So then Freddy told them all that had happened at Lakeside. Or perhaps not quite all. For if he didn't tell how he and Mr. Camphor had fallen over each other running away from the ghost, or how silly he had looked spinning over the lake like a fly on a windowpane, I don't know why you should blame him. You wouldn't have told anybody either.

The animals were disturbed to hear that Simon had probably turned up again. But as Freddy pointed out, there was nothing they could do until he had more facts to give them. He would continue his investigations; they could be ready, and when he needed their help he would send for them. "In the meantime," he said, "I'd better go see that chipmunk who had some information about Simon. Where'd you say he lived, Jinx?"

"Macy's, down on the flats," said the cat. "There's a little pond, used to be an ice pond."

"Sure, sure; I know the place," said Freddy impatiently.

"You sure you can find it? The chipmunk says there's a little clump of birches on the west side . . ."

"I told you I knew the place," Freddy said.

"Pooh, I could find my way there with my eyes shut."

The cat grinned. "Oh, yeah? Want to bet on it?"

Freddy put on his Great Detective expression, which consisted of pressing his mouth very tightly together and squinting up his eyes so that he looked suspicious and determined at the same time. He had practiced this expression before the looking glass until it was now almost perfect, and strangers were often quite terrified by it. "Certainly not!" he snapped. "Too busy for such foolishness!"

But Jinx just laughed. "You kill me, pig," he said. "Look, smooth out that face before it sets that way and I'll make a deal with you. You know that red velvet cushion I sleep on? It's just the thing to put in your big chair, now that it's busted and the springs stick into you. If you can find that pond, blindfolded, you can have the cushion."

"Look, Jinx," Freddy began, "I haven't time . . ."

"A nice, soft, thick, red velvet cushion," said Jinx. "With that in your chair, you can get your nose up over the edge of the table, instead of sitting practically on the floor and reaching up over your head to use the typewriter. As far as saving time goes, you're so smart you can get there just as quick with a blindfold on as without. Of course if you don't find the pond . . ."

Freddy made up his mind. "I'll find it all right. You don't need to think up a forfeit for me to pay."

"Yeah," said the cat. "You're a sly one. I thought you'd try that. No, if you don't find the pond, then you'll have to—let's see—you'll have to take me to the movies in Centerboro and buy me a soda afterwards."

And after thinking it over for a minute, Freddy agreed.

Chapter 7

Freddy stood in the middle of the barnyard and all the other animals stood around and watched while Jinx tied a handkerchief securely over his eyes. Then they all closed in on him and whirled him around four or five times so he would lose his sense of direction, and they changed their positions too, so their voices wouldn't come from the places where he had seen them standing. And then Jinx said: "Go!"

But Freddy was not a detective for nothing. To reach that pond he had to go out of the gate, cross the road and climb the fence on the other side, then across a shallow valley and up to another road. When he had crossed this road, he would be on the Macy farm. And although he didn't know exactly where the pond was, if he kept on in the same direction he was sure he would pass near it, and since like most animals he could smell water, he knew he wouldn't have much trouble finding it. As for starting out in the right direction, and holding to it all the way, there was nothing much to that. For what breeze there was came in light puffs always from the west; he had only to keep it on his right cheek and he couldn't go wrong.

He waited a moment until the breeze came stronger. It was on his left cheek. He turned around and started out, and there was a whispering of applause from the animals. But Jinx put a stop to that. "Hey, shut up, will you?" he said. "Of course he can find the pond if you're going to keep telling him when he's going right. You can follow along if you want to, but you keep your traps shut or we'll call the whole thing off." After that they kept still.

So Freddy went out of the gate. He crossed the road, and the ditch beyond it, and struggled through the wire fence, and then started down the gentle slope, stopping now and then until another puff of wind came against his right cheek and assured him that he was still going south. All the floor of this shallow valley was one big hayfield, so there were no gullies or trees or fences for him to run into, and he would have reached the Macy farm all right, and would probably have found the pond, too, —only just before he got to the bottom of the slope, the wind began to shift.

It shifted gradually around towards the south, each puff a little weaker and a little far-ther around, and so Freddy, as he went along, steering by the feel of it on his right cheek, shifted too. Pretty soon he was headed east, up the valley, instead of south, across it. He was at the bottom now, on level ground, so he didn't notice anything. And then for a few minutes the breeze died entirely and the air was per-fectly still.

Freddy stood perfectly still, too, waiting. He could hear the other animals breathing and moving around a little behind him, but that didn't tell him anything. Then a puff of wind came. It was from dead ahead—from the east, though of course he didn't know that. So he turned till it was on his right cheek and went on. And in a minute, sure enough, the ground began to slope up, just as he had expected. And he plodded along right back the way he had come.

Some of the animals who were following him began to giggle and poke each other, but Jinx flattened his ears and glared so ferociously that they quieted down. And Freddy went on, felt his way through the fence and across the road, and then across the Bean fence, a little way up from the gate. Up the hill past the farmyard he went, missing his own home, the pigpen, by only a few yards. Then he put his nose up in the air and sniffed. "I smell water," he said. "Better haul out that cushion, cat—it'll be mine in another few minutes."

Freddy smelt water all right, but it wasn't the Macy pond—it was the duck pond on his own farm. Alice and Emma, Mr. Bean's two white ducks, were swimming around on it, occasionally tipping up to stand on their heads in the water and search the rich mud for the kind of delicacies nobody but a duck would care to sample. Their Uncle Wesley, a pompous little duck who had come to live with them, was snoozing in the shade of a burdock leaf on the bank. He didn't hear Freddy coming, and when the blindfolded pig walked slowly up to the

"Ouch!" he yelled. "You great clumsy lummox!"

edge of the water and stopped, he stepped squarely on the duck's large flat left foot.

Uncle Wesley woke with a strangled and outraged quack. "Ouch!" he yelled. "You great clumsy lummox!"

Freddy snatched off the handkerchief. "Oh, I'm sorry," he said. "Very careless of me." He looked around. "I didn't know that Mr. Macy kept ducks down here. Very nice place. Looks very much like our own duck pond, over on the Bean farm." Then he stared hard at Uncle Wesley. "Why you—you're Uncle Wesley! What on earth are you doing down here?"

"Sir," said the duck, who was trying to recover his dignity while hopping around on one foot—not an easy thing to do; "sir, I am minding my own business, and I would recommend that you do the same."

"Well," said Freddy, "that's what I . . ."

"Pardon me," Uncle Wesley continued; "your business, whatever it is, does not include blundering up here with a silly handkerchief over your eyes and tramping all over a private citizen, who is sitting quietly in his own front yard, contemplating the beauties of nature."

"But . . ." Freddy began.

"As a private citizen," the duck went on, still

hopping about, "I have my rights and I intend to stand on them."

"Well, all right," said Freddy; "go on, do it, and quit jumping around; I can't talk to anybody who won't stand still. What did you have for lunch—grasshoppers?" He turned to Jinx. "How'd these ducks get over here anyway? How . . ." He stopped at the roar of laughter that went up from the other animals.

It took some time to explain to Freddy what had happened. And even after he realized how, guided by the shifting wind, he had walked right around in a half circle and come back to the place he had started from, he felt pretty confused. "I can't understand it," he said, looking out across the valley towards the Macy farm. "I can't be two places at once, and yet I know this is Macy's pond, and yet—yet I can see I'm here . . ."

"OK, pig," said Jinx. "You can take it from us you're here. And I can tell you where you'll be a few nights from now, too—you'll be in front of the ticket window at the Centerboro movie theatre, asking for two good seats."

Alice and Emma had swum over and were fussing around their uncle. They supported him while he hobbled down and held his injured foot in the cool water. Freddy apologized again, but the duck closed his eyes and turned his head away with as much of an expression of intense suffering as a duck can get on his face.

"Come on, Freddy," said Jinx. "That chipmunk is waiting for you. Try finding the pond with your eyes open this time. I'll go along and set you right in case you get going round in circles again." He grinned at the pig, but after that he didn't say any more about it. He was smart enough to know that you don't gain anything by crowing over your victories.

The chipmunk came out of his hole when they finally reached the pond. "About time," he said grumpily. "You'd think it was you doing me a favor, instead of vice versa and otherwise." He scowled at Freddy. "You know anybody named Mr. Eha?"

"Mr. what?" said the pig.

"Eha! Eha!" the chipmunk snapped. "Can't you understand English?"

"Maybe I could if you'd stop hiccuping," Freddy retorted. "Well, so somebody's name is Eha. What of it?"

"If you'll sit down and keep still maybe I can tell you," said the chipmunk irritably. Like all chipmunks, he spoke jerkily, stamping his feet, flicking his tail, and giving continual little jumps as if he felt pins being stuck in him. This sort of thing makes chipmunks very difficult to hold an orderly conversation with. "Day before yesterday I was up at my brother-in-law's. That road above the Bean farm—runs between Bean woods and the Big Woods. He lives there. Invited me up for his birthday. Had to take him a present, too. Cause talk if I didn't, I suppose.

"Well, I was just starting home when I saw two rats coming up the road. Don't like rats, so I hid in the stone wall. They sat down to rest under the wall, and one of them says: 'This is old Bean's property, ain't it?'

" 'Sure is,' says the other. 'He's next but one on the list, I understand.'

" 'When do we move in on old Camphor?' says the first, and the other says: 'Soon as Mr. Eha gets that hotel property. Simon wants him to take the Bean farm next, but Eha says no, we got to get Camphor's place first.'

" 'Be funny being back at Bean's,' says the first. 'Boy, won't old Simon be happy! He sure hates those Bean animals—specially that smart aleck of a pig. He says he's going to have him stuffed and set up in the front yard, as soon as Mr. Eha gets the Bean place.'

"They both snickered quite a while over that, and then they talked some more about how smart this Eha is. Seems like he's planning to get hold of all the farm property in this part of the county. But I didn't quite get how he expects to do it."

"I do," said Freddy. "This is more serious than I thought." He told the chipmunk what had happened at Lakeside. "You see, he wrecks the property and scares out the owner, and then I suppose he plans to buy it in cheap. Mrs. Filmore is broke; she'll have to sell the hotel and take what she can get for it. But look—did you get any idea about who this Eha is, or where he lives?"

"I sort of gathered that none of 'em knew. Even Simon. They only see him at night. He always wears a mask. He meets 'em somewheres, every night. And they're scared of him. Seems if they don't obey his orders he cuts off their tails. Don't suppose it hurts 'em much, but it's a terrible blow to their pride. Makes 'em look foolish—little stub of a tail." He stopped and looked startled. "Sorry," he said. "I forgot."

"No offense," said Freddy. "I never had a long tail and wouldn't know what to do with it if I did. My tail's OK. It may not impress others much, but I like it."

"H'mph," said the chipmunk. "Well, I daresay it isn't much bother." He glanced at his own elegant tail, then at Freddy's. "Well," he said, "good afternoon." And darted into his hole.

Chapter 8

When they left the Macy pond, Freddy and Jinx separated. The cat went back to the farm to tell the animals about Mr. Eha, and Freddy went on down to Centerboro, and called on Mrs. Lafayette Bingle, with whom Mrs. Filmore had gone to stay. Mrs. Bingle welcomed him warmly; he had once done a small detective job for her and she had been very grateful.

"Come in," she said. "This is an unexpected pleasure. What can I do for you?" He asked for Mrs. Filmore. "My cousin is out," she said, "but she'll be back in a few minutes."

"Well," said Freddy, "Mr. Camphor and I have discovered some things that she ought to know." And he told his story.

"Dear me," said Mrs. Bingle, "this is indeed terrible! Mr. Eha, you say? An odd name—is it Turkish? Not that it matters; we'll find out who he is when he buys the hotel."

"Yes," said Freddy, "but then it will be too late."

Mrs. Bingle looked doubtful. "Mrs. Filmore has used up her last cent, and she owes a good deal of money. She has got to sell. And in fact she has gone downtown this morning to see about it."

"Oh, dear," said Freddy; "we must get her to hold off. She . . ."

At that moment the door opened and Mrs. Filmore came in. She seemed surprised to find a pig in the parlor, but when the whole thing had been explained to her she smiled rather sadly and said: "So you really did attend Mrs. Bingle professionally, though as a detective and not as a doctor. I told her about Dr. Hopper, but she said she'd never heard of him, and we've been wondering who on earth he was."

"It's odd we didn't think of Freddy," said

Mrs. Bingle. "He has so many disguises that when Centerboro people see some stranger in town, they always wonder first if it isn't our detective, working on a case. Anyhow, we know he isn't this Mr. Eha."

"I've never heard the name," said Mrs. Filmore. "Not that it matters; I've got to sell soon, and even if you found out who he is, what could we do? Have him arrested? We couldn't prove anything."

"No, but there are other things we could do."

Mrs. Filmore shook her head. "If I get any kind of an offer I shall have to take it. As a matter of fact, when I stopped in to see Mr. Anderson, the real estate agent, he said that he had an inquiry only yesterday for a hotel property like mine. He's going to talk to this person, and then let me know."

"Who is the inquiry from?" Freddy asked.

"He wouldn't say. He said he was not at liberty to disclose the man's name."

"That sounds queer."

"Oh, I don't think so," said Mrs. Filmore. "Mr. Anderson said the person didn't want to appear in it at all. He wants Anderson to buy it and make all the arrangements. Then he'll hire a manager to open the hotel and run it. People often buy property that way."

Freddy didn't say any more, but when he left he went into the drugstore and looked in the telephone book. He looked for Anderson.

Anderson, A.G., 109 Elm	1335
Anderson, Mrs. Dimple, 17 Cranberry	2488
Anderson, Dougal, lawyer, 76 Main	3003
Anderson, Edw. Henry, rl. est., 45 Clinton	2949

"That's him," said Freddy, and rang the number.

"Mr. Anderson," he said when he had the man on the phone, "this is Horace Green, formerly proprietor of the Ocean House at Wophasset, Mass. I'm looking for a small summer hotel in this locality—want to buy it and open up this coming season. Do you know anything of the kind within, say, fifty miles?"

Mr. Anderson's hearty voice hurt Freddy's ear. "Hotel, eh? Sorry, Mr. Green. I'd like your business. But I don't know of a thing—not a blessed thing, and that's a fact."

Freddy asked a few more questions, but got nowhere, and then hung up. "Funny," he thought. "If Mrs. Filmore wants him to sell Lakeside, why wouldn't he tell me about it? I don't get it."

Freddy made a few more short calls in Centerboro and then got a bite to eat at Dixon's Diner, so that it was almost dark when he finally got back to Mr. Camphor's. The breeze had gone down with the sun and the lake was like glass as Bannister started to paddle him across the lake.

"I don't see how you keep the canoe going straight when you just paddle on one side," Freddy said.

"One can do several things to keep it straight, sir," said the butler. "The twist at the end of the stroke swings it back to the side you're paddling on. Scooping your stroke under the canoe will turn it to that side, and so will taking the stroke with the inside edge of the paddle twisted a little towards you."

"But you paddle so silently. I thought to do that you had to bring back the blade for the next stroke under water."

"You can do that," Bannister said. "But if you put the paddle in and take it out quietly, and then when you bring it back for the next stroke, hold the blade a little up, so the water runs up the shaft instead of dripping off—see? On a still night like tonight, those drops make a lot of noise."He shook a few from the paddle and they tinkled.

Freddy didn't say any more. We're gliding, he thought—gliding like a ghost. Through space, with empty sky above and below us. You can't even tell which is up and which down, for you can't see the water. There are only stars, above and below the boat.

From somewhere across the lake came a faint hollow thump or knock, and at once Bannister stopped paddling. "Did you hear that?" he said in a low voice. "Someone hit a paddle against the gunwale of a boat."

They listened, but it didn't come again, and Bannister went on, but more slowly. "Why only once?" he said. "If it's someone rowing or paddling carelessly, you'd hear it again."

"Well, what of it?" said Freddy. "Lots of people must use this lake."

"Summer people," Bannister said. "But it's too early for them. There's nobody at the Boy Scout camp down at the outlet. If it was an hour or two earlier, it might be somebody trying to get a look at a deer. I don't say it's any of our business, but under the circumstances, let's get in under the shore where they won't have us against the starlit water." He paddled on, swiftly and noiselessly.

Halfway between Jones's Bay and Lakeside they slid in under the loom of the trees that overhung the water and sat silently waiting. A very faint red glow came from somewhere near Stony Point.

"Mr. Camphor hasn't got a very big fire," Freddy whispered.

"Better not whisper, sir," said Bannister. "A whisper carries farther on a still night than if you just speak low. —Ha! Look out there— down the lake a little!"

At first Freddy couldn't see anything but the reflection of the starlit sky in the water. Then at one spot the stars quivered and shook. Something had disturbed the smooth lake surface. And then a patch of darkness, blotting out the starshine, moved across the water. It glided in towards the Lakeside dock.

They saw a flashlight flicker; someone was walking up the dock towards the hotel. "We'd better get Mr. Camphor," Freddy murmured, and Bannister's paddle slid into the water. The canoe swung round and moved back towards Stony Point.

Mr. Camphor walked down to meet them as

they beached the canoe. "My goodness, you're late," he said. "But Bannister, why did you come over? How are you going to get back?"

"Not so loud!" said Freddy. "Our friend is up at the hotel. Look, I want to do a little sleuthing." He took off the coonskin cap and handed it to the butler. "You be Dr. Hopper for a while. Sit by the fire with Mr. Camphor, but not so close that anybody can see you very well. I'll be back." And he sneaked off up the path to Lakeside.

He crept around to the back of the hotel and crouched under the office window. There was no light inside. The shade was still pulled down, but through the broken pane he could hear a voice speaking in a sharp whisper. "I don't intend to tell you where Ezra is, my friend. He's locked up in a safe place. Nothing will happen to him if you obey my orders."

"Oh now, Mr. Eha, sir," said an oily voice which Freddy recognized as that of his old enemy Simon; "it isn't that we don't trust *you;* it's that you don't trust *us.* We rats are for you a hundred per cent. We've done everything you've asked us to . . ."

"I don't trust anybody," the whisperer interrupted. "As long as you obey my orders, I'll supply you with food—better food, I may point out, than you've ever had before in your lives. And Ezra will be well treated. But if you fail to carry out orders—well, you know what will happen to him."

"But why are you suspicious of us?" Simon whined. "We have been loyal . . ."

"I don't expect loyalty; I expect obedience. This is a business arrangement. Each of us has agreed to do certain things. And I intend that you shall carry out your side of the bargain.

"But that's enough about that," he said. "Our job here is about done. Mrs. Filmore has been driven away. A day or two more and the hotel will belong to me. Tonight I will take you back to your cottage. Tomorrow night we go to Camphor's. We'll start on that place at once. There's nobody there but old Camphor, his butler, and the two old maid aunts. We'll proceed in the same way—do enough damage to make the house unlivable, and scare 'em out with the usual ghost stuff. It should take about six weeks. Then we'll move on to the Bean farm."

"Ha! The Bean farm!" Simon snarled. "Ever since that fat-faced Freddy and his friends drove us off the place I've been waiting to get even. I swore I'd come back some day and live in that barn."

"You do what you're told and you'll get the barn," said Mr. Eha. "I've promised you that. But we're wasting time. I've got to get rid of this camping party. They're too much interested in what's been going on at the hotel."

"If you take my advice you'll shoot 'em," said Simon. "They'd be easy to pick off, sitting around their fire."

"Your advice is stupid," the other whispered. "A shooting would bring the state troopers up here. They'd talk to Mrs. Filmore, and policemen don't believe in ghosts, particularly ghosts that shoot off guns. Now you get the rest of your gang and go on down to the dock and wait for me."

"You going to leave those things here?" said Simon. "Suppose Camphor comes in here and finds them?"

"After the scare I gave him last night?" said Mr. Eha. "He wouldn't come into this room again after dark for a thousand dollars. Get along."

Freddy left the window and crept around the far side of the hotel until he reached a corner from which he could see both the front door and the shore end of the dock. Pretty soon there was a scrabbling and scampering on the porch, and he could just make out the dark forms of the rats as they came out of the door and hurried down to Mr. Eha's canoe. He thought there were about twenty of them. A minute later a figure appeared in the doorway. Even though Freddy knew what it was, it was pretty terrifying. It was draped in something white that fluttered in a very ghostly manner. But the head was the worst. It was the head of some kind of demon, with great round eyes and long tusks, and it glowed with a sort of smoky luminosity.

Freddy shuddered in spite of himself. "Luminous paint, I suppose," he thought. "Golly, wait till Mr. Camphor and Bannister see that goggling at them! They'll just give one squawk and fall right over on their faces." He giggled nervously. "Boy, I'd like to see 'em!"

But when the figure moved on down the path toward the camp, he went up the steps and into the house. For if Mr. Eha had left something in the office, now was his chance to see what it was.

Of course he couldn't see a thing. The office was pitch black, and it wasn't much fun feeling

Freddy was good and scared.

around in the darkness from which that hor-
rifying figure had come. As a banker, Freddy
didn't take much stock in ghosts, but as a poet,
he had a lively imagination, and he began to
think of all the things that he might find: of
fingers that might tap him confidentially on the
shoulder, of cold hands that might clasp his
wrist, of thick, oily groans that might come
from that far corner. Then he fell over something and gave a groan himself, for there was
a thump, and jaws snapped shut on his leg.

Freddy was good and scared. He thought of
steel traps. He thought of alligators. He lay
there for a moment and cold perspiration ran
down his back under the heavy wool shirt. But
the jaws didn't do anything, and they weren't
very tight. He drew his leg out cautiously, and
then felt around on the floor. A suitcase! It
had been open when he fell over it, and the lid
had come down and caught him.

Freddy felt foolish, and you can't feel foolish and afraid at the same time. He got up and
went through the suitcase, feeling of every arti-
cle. There were some pieces of cloth, and a
small bottle, and several things that he couldn't
identify. There were two false faces, and remembering the advice he had once given some-

one—or someone had once given him—to walk
right up to a ghost and say Boo! he took one of
them out and put it on. On the back of a chair
was a coat—it was certainly Mr. Eha's, but the
pockets were empty except for a few slips of
paper, which Freddy took. He didn't have any
matches, so he couldn't see what they were. He
felt of the coat, but the cloth was—well, just
cloth. There was nothing he could recognize
it by if he saw it again. And yet, wasn't there
something he could do, he wondered, so that
if he ever did see it again, he would know that
the wearer was Mr. Eha?

"Oh, dear," he thought, "if I only had a
knife I could make a little cut somewhere, maybe on the back where he wouldn't notice it.
Then if we just watched for that coat . . ."
He felt in all his pockets. Some string. Half a
candy bar. And what was this in the upper shirt
pocket? "Good gracious," he said, "three mothballs! No wonder this shirt never gets the smell
aired out of it." And he was just about to throw
them away when he had an idea, and he slipped
the mothballs into the outside breast pocket of
Mr. Eha's coat.

Chapter 9

If Mr. Eha had been a real ghost, he could have flitted from Lakeside down to Stony Point and scared Mr. Camphor and Bannister into roaring fits before Freddy had finished exploring the suitcase. But being just a man wrapped up in a sheet and wearing a false face, he had to go pretty slowly along the narrow trail. Freddy overtook him just as he came within sight of the campfire and stopped behind a tree to look over the ground.

Freddy stopped too. The fire had died down

to a bed of coals, and Mr. Camphor, who of course had had nothing to eat all day, was mixing flapjacks with the flour Bannister had brought in the canoe. He put a spoonful of batter in the frying pan and held it over the coals, just as Mr. Eha moved out from his tree.

Bannister was sitting on a log a little back from the fire, and when he caught sight of that ghastly figure, he didn't make a sound, he just fell backwards off the log and lay there with his hands over his face.

Mr. Camphor saw the movement from the corner of his eye. "Tired?" he asked, and flipped the pancake and caught it neatly. "Why don't you spread out a blanket and take a nap?"

Bannister didn't reply. Mr. Camphor waited till the flapjack was done, slid it onto a plate, and spooned more batter into the pan. Then as he looked around to see why the butler didn't answer, he saw the ghost.

"Wow!" he shouted, and jumped up. But he kept hold of the frying pan, though it shook in his hand. He wasn't so much scared as startled, for he knew this time that there was a man behind the mask.

"Ha!" he said. "A denizen of the underworld! A what-you-may-call-em from the deep dark forest. Approach, what-you-may-call-em, and give me your message." He turned towards Bannister. "Hey, Banni . . . that is, Dr. Hopper, we've got company."

Mr. Eha had no intention of coming closer to the light of the fire. He was probably pretty disappointed at the failure of his scheme. Crouching behind his bush, Freddy tried hard not to giggle. "This Eha," he thought, "isn't very bright. I suppose he figured they'd just dash for the canoe and paddle off."

But Mr. Eha stood his ground. There wasn't much else he could do. If he tried to run, in that sheet, with a heavy mask over his head, they'd catch him in ten seconds. He began to fumble under the sheet—and Freddy got ready to jump out. Mr. Eha probably had a gun.

But he didn't produce a gun. He took a step forward, and said in a sharp whisper: "Beware, rash mortal! The powers of darkness are all around you. Hark, do you not hear them muttering together? Begone, ere worse befall you."

"Very fancy language," said Mr. Camphor. "And as nothing has befell yet, why not sit down and have a flapjack with us?"

"Needs must when the devil drives," came a shaky voice from behind the log.

He threw the flapjack—plop!—straight into the demon's face.

"Ha, do you think so, Doctor?" Mr. Camphor said. "We'll look into that one." He got up and walked slowly towards Mr. Eha, shaking the frying pan a little to loosen the half-cooked flapjack. "Come along, try these," he said. "I assure you they're very good." And then suddenly with an overhand flip of his arm, he threw the flapjack—plop!—straight into the demon's face.

Now the under side of the flapjack was toasted a light brown, but the upper side was still uncooked, and it plastered the eyes and nose of the mask with sticky wet dough. Mr. Eha gave a muffled growl and clawed at the dough and then Mr. Camphor threw himself on him, and Bannister rose from behind the log and brought him to the ground with a remarkable flying tackle.

"First down for our side," Mr. Camphor panted, as the sheeted figure struggled desperately to get away.

"Give the devil his due, sir," said Bannister. "And I'll hold his legs while you do it."

"I know a better one," Mr. Camphor gasped. "The devil's not as black as he's painted. We'll have a look and see. Wait till I get . . . mask off."

There was plenty of fight in Mr. Eha, but he couldn't get it out—he was wrapped too tightly in the sheet. Mr. Camphor got a hand free and ripped off the false face but under it was a black mask, with eyeholes, that fitted over Eha's forehead and eyes and nose. And before Mr. Camphor could get that off, Freddy appeared.

Now Freddy had forgotten that he still wore the false face that he'd found in the suitcase, and he didn't at all realize what he looked like when he came tearing out to the rescue. Mr. Camphor had been prepared for a man disguised as a ghost. But when he and Bannister looked up and saw this undersized creature with the head of a gorilla rushing apparently to attack them, it is not surprising that they jumped up and backed away in terror. And then before Freddy could figure out what was the matter and take the false face off, Mr. Eha had scrambled to his feet, and the last they saw of him that night was the flicker of a flashlight and a vanishing flutter of white down the trail that led to Lakeside.

Chapter 10

At the first pale glimmer of dawn Freddy crawled out of his sleeping bag. Mr. Camphor, in the other bag, and Bannister, rolled up in a blanket, seemed to be having a snoring competition. Freddy listened a minute and awarded the prize to Bannister—his snores weren't as loud, but they had more variety. Then he went down and washed in the lake.

The light was growing, and the eastern sky began to glow red, as if some giant had opened a furnace door behind the hills. Freddy sat down and watched it and sniffed the fresh morning smells of water and pine and spruce and damp earth, and he thought: "My goodness, I didn't know camping was so nice. But am I hungry! Don't suppose I ought to start the fire till they get up though. Maybe I won't be so hungry if I make up a poem."

So he started one. It went to the tune of Mandalay. He sang it:

By the old hotel at Lakeside, looking southward
*   'cross the sea,*
There's a bright campfire a'burning, and I
*   know it burns for me.*
For the wind is in the pine trees, and the mur-
*   muring needles say:*
Come you back, you pig detective—come you
*   back to Jones's Bay;*
*   Come you baaaack to Jones's Ba-a-a-ay!*

Then he went on with the chorus, a little louder. And gradually—as sometimes happens to poets—his hunger for breakfast got mixed up in the poem, so that the chorus went like this:

Oh, the road to Jones's Bay! Where the flying
*   flapjacks play!*
You can hear the bacon sizzling from your bed
*   at break of day.*

On the road to Jones's Ba-hay, we will sing and
    shout hooray;
A-and when your breakfast's ready, they will
    bring it o-on a tray!

"Well, well," he said, "I guess I'd better do
something to take my mind off my stomach."
There was a cold flapjack left over from last
night lying on a plate beside the fireplace. He
picked it up and took a bite out of it, but even
the sharpest appetite will blunt itself on a cold
flapjack. He started to throw it in the lake, then
put it in the frying pan and practiced flipping
it. He thought he would practice until he could
make it turn three complete somersaults without missing the pan when it came down, and
would then astonish Mr. Camphor with his
skill.

But after ten minutes he had dropped the
flapjack so many times that it was about worn
out. And the snoring competition in the lean-to
was still going on. He thought: "My gracious,
I'm neglecting my detective duties. They won't
wake up for another hour. I'd better go up and
snoop around the hotel." So he did.

It wasn't very good snooping. The office and
the lounge offered no clues. It wasn't until he
started down the dock that he found the hand-

kerchief. An ordinary white handkerchief with EHA marked on one corner in indelible ink. "So Eha is really his name," he thought. "But what does that get me? I still don't know where he lives." And he was thinking this over when a little squeaky voice said somewhere: "Help!"

Freddy looked all around but couldn't see anybody. "Where are you?" he called.

"In the boathouse."

There were a number of canoes and rowboats on racks in the boathouse. Back of them, and hung from a hook in the ceiling was a big rat trap—a square wire cage with a spring door. In it was a rat.

Rats look a good deal alike,—and so for that matter do squirrels and pigs and elephants. But when you get to know them, you find that they differ in looks as much as people do. Freddy had known Simon and his family pretty well, and he recognized this rat at once as Simon's son, Ezra, the one that Mr. Eha was holding as hostage for his family's good behavior.

As soon as he saw Freddy, Ezra sat up and put his forepaws against the wire and began begging to be let out.

"Now wait a minute," said Freddy, realizing that the rat hadn't recognized him, "if Mrs. Filmore caught you in this trap, I can't let you out without her permission."

"Mrs. Filmore didn't have anything to do with it," Ezra squeaked. "Who are you, anyway? I never saw you before."

"Well, I know who you are," said Freddy. "If I'm not mistaken, you're closely related to a rat that lived in my barn all one winter. Old Simon. Fine, sturdy old fellow, Simon; we got to be great pals. You look enough like him to be his son."

"I am his son. And if you let me out—I tell you he's offered a big reward for me and you'll get it all," he said eagerly. "Look, you tell me where you live and he'll bring it to you. To-morrow."

"H'm," said Freddy, "you're a better liar than I am, Ezra." He took off his cap. "Know me now?"

"Oh, gosh!" said Ezra. "Freddy! Oh, gee, I'm sunk now all right." And he lay down on the floor of the cage.

"Maybe so," said the pig, and he picked up the trap and started down the trail to camp. "If you tell me what we want to know, maybe we'll let you go."

The two men were up and getting breakfast.

Ezra put his forepaws against the wire and began begging to be let out.

They didn't think much of Freddy's capture. "He's just one of the gang," said Mr. Camphor. "Now if you'd captured them all. . . . Sit down and have some coffee."

"He's Simon's son," said Freddy. "My guess is that in the hurry of getting away last night they forgot all about him down in the boat-house. But Mr. Eha doesn't want to lose him, because Ezra is the only hold he has over Simon, and he needs Simon's help for his scheme. I bet you anything he comes back for Ezra to-night."

"And then what do we do?" said Mr. Camphor. "Chase him around in the woods and make faces at each other again?"

"The trouble is," Freddy said, "that we don't know who Eha is. Maybe Simon knows, but I don't believe that the other rats do. I don't think Ezra knows anything. Eh, Ez?" he said, glancing at the cage.

The rat made a face at him.

"But I'm pretty sure he lives in Centerboro," Freddy went on, "because—look at these." And he drew out the slips of paper he had found in Eha's coat. They were checks for meals that someone had eaten at Dixon's Diner. "He must eat at the diner often," Freddy said, "because

he wouldn't be able to sneak every check he got
into his pocket and walk out without paying,
which is what he must have done. For how else
could he have got them? You know what?—I'm
going down to Centerboro and try to find him
this afternoon."

"Well, even if you did find out who he was,"
said Mr. Camphor, "the police wouldn't believe any such story. Rats and ghosts! They'd
just give you the old heave-ho."

"Sure. We won't bother the police. We'll just
bother Mr. Eha. You leave it to the old reliable
firm—they know how to handle crooks.—Hey!"
he said suddenly. "What goes on?" And he
pointed across the lake.

Far across where the lawns of the Camphor
estate made a pale green line on the distant
shore, something white fluttered.

"Someone waving a tablecloth," said Bannister.

"Must be something wrong," said Mr. Camphor, getting up. "Better go see."

Freddy sat in the middle of the canoe with
the rat trap on his knees, and under the strong
strokes of Mr. Camphor and the butler the
canoe cut sharply through the blue and silver
ripples. As they came closer the lawns widened

out, the house and the dock and the trees grew larger, and a group at the edge of the water grew more distinct. "Ha!" Freddy exclaimed. "Reinforcements!" And there indeed were nearly all the animals from the Bean farm— Mrs. Wiggins and one of her sisters, Mrs. Wogus, Charles and Henrietta, Robert and Georgie, the dogs, Jinx, and even the four mice: Eek and Quik and Eeeny and Cousin Augustus. "And my gracious!" said Freddy. "There's Mr. Bean too!"

It was indeed Mr. Bean who stepped forward and held the canoe for them as they climbed out.

"Very pleased to see you, sir," said Mr. Camphor, shaking hands with him. "I take it you've heard about the plans this villain Eha has for getting hold of our property, and have brought these animals up to defeat him."

" 'Tain't my doing," said Mr. Bean. "Mrs. Bean, she heard about it somewheres." He frowned slightly. He was kind of old-fashioned about having animals talk; it made him uneasy, and he always said animals should be seen and not heard. So Freddy and his friends seldom said anything to him; if there was anything important they told Mrs. Bean. He never asked her where such information came from. But of course he knew, and was pretty proud, secretly, of having such clever animals.

Mr. Bean went on: "Mrs. Bean says: 'Mr. B.,' says she, 'don't you let those animals go up to Camphor's alone.' 'Well, Mrs. B.,' says I, 'I figure our Freddy is running this show, and I don't ever interfere with him. If he wants my help he knows he can ask for it and get it.' 'But 'cordin' to what I hear,' she says, 'this rapscallion Eha is going to try to get our place next.' 'And I'll be ready for him,' I says; 'but,' says I, 'if Mr. Camphor and this hotel woman's in trouble, maybe it's only neighborly for me to traipse along. If they don't want me, they can tell me so.' "

"And we're very grateful," said Mr. Camphor, seizing Mr. Bean's hand and shaking it again. "Come up on the terrace and we'll talk it over. Bannister, the twenty-five cent cigars."

The animals had stood quietly listening. They were bursting with questions for Freddy, but they knew their talk would disturb Mr. Bean and they respected his wishes for they were very fond of him. As the men turned away, they gathered around the pig, but before they could say anything a shrill voice called: "Jim-

son! Jimson Camphor! What are all those animals doing here?" And they saw Miss Minerva's
gaunt figure striding angrily down towards
them.

"Oh, just some friends of mine," said Mr.
Camphor. "Aunt Minerva, may I present Mr.
William Bean?"

"How do," she said shortly. "Are you the—
the manager of this menagerie? These are
private grounds; you can't bring these animals
in here."

"Come, come, Aunt," said Mr. Camphor,
"after all, they're my grounds, and—"

Mr. Bean laid a hand on his arm and winked
one eye. Then he turned to Miss Minerva and
said with a courtly bow: "My dear lady, I assure you that we are here only to serve you. To
protect you from the villain who is plotting to
defraud your nephew of his fine property."

"What villain?" said Miss Minerva. "I know
nothing about any plot."

"Well, there is one," put in Mr. Camphor,
and he told her about Mr. Eha and his schemes.

"Folderol!" she exclaimed. "I never heard
such nonsense. You men are all the same:
scared of your own shadows and seeing bogies

behind every bush. Where is this Eha? Let me talk to him."

"That's just the trouble, ma'am," said Mr. Bean. "We don't know who he is, or where or when he may strike. However, you have requested me to leave. And a Bean, ma'am, could never refuse the request of so charming a lady. Come, animals!"

The animals of course couldn't move. They stared at Mr. Bean and their eyes almost fell out of their sockets. For this was a Mr. Bean they didn't know. These polished manners, these lavish compliments—they could hardly believe their ears.

Miss Minerva's face relaxed into what might have been the beginning of a smile, and she looked sidelong at Mr. Bean. "Well," she said slowly, "if you put it that way . . ."

"I do put it that way, ma'am," he replied firmly. "That is exactly how I put it. A charming and cultured lady like yourself—who am I to refuse your lightest request?"

Miss Minerva really smiled now. "Flatterer!" she said, and squeaked faintly with pleasure, and she continued to look curiously at him.

But nobody ever found out anything about

Mr. Bean by looking at him. Behind those whiskers he might have been handsome or plain, he might be smiling or scornful—nobody ever knew, not even Mrs. Bean.

"Come, animals," he said again.

"Wait!" said Miss Minerva. "Perhaps—perhaps I have been too hasty. Come," she said, putting her hand through his arm, "let us go up on the terrace and you can tell me more of this plot."

"Well, great day in the morning!" said Mr. Camphor, staring after them.

Mrs. Wiggins laughed her comfortable laugh. "I told you you'd get along better with her if you'd pay her a compliment once in a while," she said.

Mr. Camphor closed his eyes a moment in intense thought. Then he opened them and said to the butler: "Music hath charms to soothe the savage breast. I think that proverb about covers it, eh, Bannister?"

"No doubt, sir, if you can classify that voice as music. And on the other hand, there's this one: Fine words butter no parsnips."

"Ha," said Mr. Camphor; "Aunt Minerva's no parsnip, but I'd say he buttered her up all right."

The animals had surrounded Freddy and were talking and laughing and congratulating him on his capture of Ezra. "Hurrah for Freddy!" they shouted. "He brings 'em back alive! Freddy always gets his animal." Jinx pushed through the crowd. He put a paw on the trap and peered in at the rat, who squeezed back into a corner. "What you got in this birdcage, Freddy? Pretty little thing, ain't he? Can he sing?"

"Like a thrush, Jinx; like a thrush," said Freddy. "Want to hear him? Give us a song, Ez."

"Aw, you think you're awful funny," Ezra snarled. "You just wait till Mr. Eha gets here, you big stuck-up— Ouch!" he squeaked. "You quit that!" For Jinx had reached through the wires and cuffed his ear.

"You hadn't ought to do that, Jinx," said Mrs. Wiggins.

"Well then let him quit calling names, the grimy sneak," said Jinx.

The rat sneered at him. "Who's calling names now? If I wasn't in a cage, you wouldn't talk so big."

"Oh, shut up, both of you!" said Freddy. "Now look, animals. Mr. Eha is going to make plenty of trouble for all of us if we don't stop him. Once we know who he is, we can pepper his hash all right. So I'm going down to Centerboro and find out. Georgie, I need your help; will you go with me?"

"Gee, you bet I will!" said the little brown dog.

"All right. We'll see if Bannister will drive us down, to save time. And the rest of you—my goodness, I'm glad you came up today; you're going to be needed. Until I get back, the main thing is to see that Ezra doesn't get away. And keep an eye out for Simon and the rest of the gang. I have a hunch they're around here somewhere, and they might try a rescue."

Chapter 11

Freddy didn't know just what he might get into in Centerboro, and he thought it would be better if nobody recognized him. So he borrowed a derby hat and a dark suit from Mr. Camphor, who was really just about his size. With these on, and carrying the medicine case marked Henry Hopper M.D., he could easily have been taken for an undersized medical man, just going out on a call.

He gave Georgie his instructions and posted him at the door of Dixon's Diner, and then he went in and sat at the counter and ordered a cup of cocoa. It wasn't dinner time yet, so there were no other customers.

Mr. Dixon was a little round worried looking man. He put the cocoa in front of Freddy and said: "Stranger in town?"

"What do you think?" said Freddy, and took off the derby.

"Why, you're Freddy!" said Mr. Dixon. "Good gracious me—you investigating another crime?"

"Sssssssh!" said Freddy, putting the derby back on. "Not a word! Yes, a very serious crime, and I think maybe you can help me. Ever hear of a Mr. Eha?"

"Eha?" said Mr. Dixon. "That ain't a name. It's a laugh, ain't it, like Ha-ha! or O-ho-ho!?"

"It may not be his real name," Freddy said. "But I can tell you something else about him: he's been coming in here and eating, and then sneaking out without paying his check. I found these unpaid checks in his pocket." Freddy spread them out on the counter.

"I've got some customers that do that," said Mr. Dixon. "I guess I don't watch them as carefully as I should." He examined the checks. "Let's see—corned beef and cabbage on the eighteenth—that was Friday. Now who had corned beef Friday? Judge Willey did, but he wouldn't skip without paying. So did Mr. Beller. H'm. Let's try another—there's too many of 'em like corned beef. Here, now—pigs' knuckles and sauer . . ." He broke off suddenly and slipped the check under the others. "Let's—er, let's see this one," he said hastily. "The twenty-first, Monday; a double order of fresh caviare. Ah ha! I know who had that! It was—" He stopped short again. "No," he said. "No, I can't tell you who that was."

"You mean you won't."

"Look, Freddy," said Mr. Dixon, lowering his voice, although there was no one else in the diner, "there's some folks I can't afford to have mad at me. I know who this is. He does it a lot. But I dassen't say anything to him. I let him get away with it rather than have a fuss. And if you'll take my advice, you'll lay off him too. He's a tough baby; he'd shoot you as soon as look at you."

Freddy knew he wasn't going to get anything more out of Mr. Dixon—the man was too scared of Mr. Eha. "Maybe you're right," he said. "Let's skip it. I think I . . ." He swung round on his stool. Outside, Georgie was barking—three barks, then two; bow-wow-wow, bow-wow, bow-wow-wow, bow-wow. "Whoops!" said Freddy, and grabbed his medicine case and dashed out of the door.

Main Street was full of people, but there was Georgie, following a tall man in a dark suit. And as Freddy caught up, he realized that a strong smell of mothballs was also following the tall man.

The dog dropped back when he saw Freddy. "You know who he is?" he asked.

"Never saw him before. We'll follow along and see; he certainly smells right."

"I think he might have come in on the eleven o'clock bus," said the dog. "He came from that way."

They followed him to a house on Elm Street before which a lot of cars were standing. Other people were coming up the street and turning in there, and Freddy motioned Georgie to wait by the gate and followed the man up the steps and to the door, which was opened by a maid in a little cap and apron. They went into the hall, side by side. The maid took the man's hat from him, and then held out her hand for Freddy's derby. And Freddy realized that he couldn't take it off. If he did, he would be recognized, and even if he wasn't thrown out, everybody would know that an uninvited detective had got in.

Looking through the doorway into the parlor, Freddy saw a lot of people all standing around laughing and talking at the top of their lungs, and at the far end flowers and potted palms were banked up. The man went in and began shaking hands with people. And the maid said sharply: "Your hat, sir?"

"I'm a—a Quaker," said Freddy quickly. "You ought to know, my girl, that Quakers never take their hats off in the house. Look at Benjamin Franklin."

"Where?" said the girl, peering into the other room.

"Skip it," said Freddy. "Look here, wasn't that Mr. Alfred Beagle that came in with me?"

"No sir, that was Mr. Platt, the bride's uncle."

"Lives on upper Dugan Street?"

"No, sir; he came from Tushville for the wedding."

The maid turned away to open the door for some other guests, and Freddy watched Mr. Platt. "Wish I could get my hand in that coat pocket," he thought. "I wonder if he really is

Mr. Eha? He smells pretty strong for just three mothballs. I've got to get into that room, but I can't with this hat on." Then he had an idea, and when the maid's back was turned he darted quickly up the stairs.

In the upstairs hall he listened. There were voices in one room; he slid by the door and popped into the one next to it. It was empty. He shut the door and listened, and as he did so, he heard someone start to play the wedding march on a piano, and then the people in the other room came out and started downstairs. "I wonder," he said to himself, "what's in that closet?"

Five minutes later Freddy came downstairs. He wore a dress with big roses all over it which he had pulled right on over Mr. Camphor's suit. Instead of the derby, which, with the medicine case, he had dropped out of the open window, he wore a large floppy garden hat. The wedding ceremony had started; nobody paid any attention to him as he teetered into the parlor in his high-heeled shoes and worked his way slowly over towards where Mr. Platt was standing.

The ceremony went on. A tall woman, standing beside him, bent down and whispered: "Doesn't Janey make a lovely bride?"

Five minutes later, Freddy came downstairs.

"Never saw her look lovelier," Freddy whispered back truthfully.

The tall woman sniffed and touched her eyes with her handkerchief. "So sad, I think, weddings," she said.

Freddy thought he'd better sniff too, as most of the women in the room seemed to be doing it. Unfortunately, his handkerchief was in his pants pocket, and he couldn't get at it without causing a lot of notice. But two or three of the guests were now crying pretty hard, so he gave a couple of good loud sobs in order not to be conspicuous.

And then the ceremony was over, and the people began milling around, and everybody was gay again. Freddy couldn't figure it out. But he didn't have any time to try. He followed Mr. Platt, who pushed through the crowd and kissed the bride.

"Oh, Uncle Joe," she said, "I was so afraid you wouldn't come! When you wrote that you didn't have a decent suit to wear—goodness, you could have come in your overalls—you know it wouldn't make any difference to me."

"Didn't have to," said Mr. Platt. "Fred Bullock lent me this suit—it's the one he was married in, and hasn't been out of the trunk since.

Kind of a wedding suit, I guess you'd call it. We just slid the mothballs out of it and slid me into it, and here I am."

"Oh, that's what I smell!" she said. "I thought it was some new kind of soap."

"We didn't have time to air it much," said Mr. Platt. "I kind of like the smell myself."

"Well," she said, "I don't. But no matter how you smell, you'll always be my favorite uncle."

"Darn it," Freddy thought, "this can't be Eha either. I'd better get out of here." But before he could slip away, the bride had flung her arms around his neck and kissed him on the cheek. "Oh, mother," she said, "wasn't it lovely? But why this dress?—I thought you were going to wear the other . . ." She broke off and pushed him away. "Why, you're not my mother!" she exclaimed.

Freddy realized what had happened. The dress he had got into upstairs must be one belonging to the girl's mother. He'd better do something quick! "Sssssh!" he whispered. "Not a word here! Meet me upstairs in five minutes and I'll explain."

He got away while she was still thinking over what he had said. But he didn't go upstairs. He went down cellar. In the little laundry he stripped off the hat and dress. There was a window over the tubs; he climbed up on the tub rim and unlatched it. And there, right outside and within reach, were his derby and the medicine case.

In another minute or so he would have been outside with them. But someone was coming down the cellar stairs. And while pigs are swift and agile on level ground, climbing is not their stuff. Freddy reached out and grabbed the derby, put a dent in it, crammed it on the back of his head, and when a large woman in an apron who might have been the cook came into the laundry, he was kneeling with his back to her, examining the waste pipe under the tub.

"Well!" she said. "How'd you get in here?"

"Same way you did—down them stairs," said Freddy in a hoarse voice. "Look, missis; there ain't anything the matter with that there drain. Why don't you make sure it's plugged before you go callin' me up? I'm a busy man."

"What are you talking about?" said the woman. "Nobody called you to fix any drain."

"Certainly did. Said hurry up over to 83 Elm Street and . . ."

"This is 22 Elm Street," she interrupted.

"What?" said Freddy, starting up. "Lordy,

lordy, how'd I get in here? I got to get over to 83—they'll skin me alive for taking so long." And he pushed past the woman and up the stairs.

Outside, he picked up his medicine case and met Georgie at the gate. "Wrong man," he said. "We've got to get back to the diner."

"OK," said the dog. "Wipe that lipstick off your face first."

"Lipstick?" said Freddy. "Oh, I must have got that when the bride thought I was her mother."

"She thought you were her mother? With a derby hat on?" said Georgie. Of course he hadn't seen Freddy in the woman's dress and hat. And he began to giggle. "Don't give me that stuff! And don't give me any bride, either. I saw you through the cellar window. Boy, if Jinx ever gets hold of that you'll never hear the last of it. Kissed by the cook! I bet she thought you were cute!"

"Well, it wasn't the cook," said Freddy. "And if you go making up any stories, I'll tell 'em about the time that little girl that visited the Beans tied a pink ribbon around your stomach and talked baby talk to you. 'Oh, oo *twe-e-et* ickle itsy-bitsy pupsy wups! I kiss'm and hug'm and kiss'm and hug'm.' Wasn't that it?"

"OK," said Georgie. "You win. I didn't see a thing."

It was about noon now, and people were beginning to go into the diner to get their dinner. Freddy stood across the street and watched Georgie, who took up his post beside the door. As each new arrival turned in, the dog would run up to him, wagging his tail. Nearly everyone would say a word to him, or stoop to pat his head, and he had a chance to get a good sniff at their pockets. He smelt a lot of different things —tobacco, peppermint, peanuts, hair tonic; Mr. Beller smelt of fried onions, Judge Willey— rather surprisingly—of bubble gum. But no mothballs—until Mr. Anderson, the real estate man, went in. Georgie took one sniff and ran across the street to Freddy. "Got him," he said. "What do we do now?"

Freddy said: "That's funny. He's about the right height for Mr. Eha, but he's an important citizen. Doesn't seem like the kind that would be playing silly ghost tricks."

"That's your problem," said the dog. "He smells of mothballs, that's all I know."

"We have to investigate him, then," said Freddy. "If he's our man, there are three mothballs in the upper outside pocket of that coat."

"When he comes out," said Georgie, "suppose I run between his legs and trip him up, and then old Dr. Hopper comes along and feels him over for broken bones, eh?"

"Sure. I could feel of his heart to see if it's still beating. That pocket is right over his heart. That's an idea, Georgie."

They had to wait about half an hour. Then as Mr. Anderson came out and started up the street, Georgie darted after him. Freddy followed more slowly. The dog trotted along beside Mr. Anderson, waiting for a chance to trip him. But Mr. Anderson did not like dogs. He turned and aimed a kick at Georgie which would certainly have broken a rib or two if it had landed square. But Georgie ducked, and the toe of the shoe caught him a glancing blow on the shoulder that shot him out into the street. Mr. Anderson just walked on.

Georgie picked himself up and came back to Freddy. "No use feeling of that guy's heart," he said. "He hasn't got any. The big bully, he might have killed me."

"I guess we'll have to be more careful," Freddy said. "He plays kind of rough. We'll wait a while and then go up to his place. I've got an idea."

Chapter 12

Mr. Anderson's office was in his house, on Clinton Street. Georgie hid behind a bush with yellow flowers on it in the yard, and Freddy went up and rang the bell. When no one answered, he pushed the door open and walked in. The office was on the left. A sign on its door said: "Back at 3 P.M." Freddy said: "Well, well," thoughtfully, and a woman came out of a door at the end of the hall and said: "You want to see Mr. Anderson? He's taking his nap now and can't be disturbed. Come back at three."

"Nonsense!" said Freddy sharply. "I'm Dr. Hopper. Where's the patient?"

The woman said: "There's nobody sick here."

"If he isn't sick, why did he send for me? And why isn't he in his office?" said Freddy.

"He takes a nap every afternoon after dinner, that's why. You ought to know that."

"I'm a doctor, not a mind reader," said Freddy. And he thought: "Takes a nap every day, eh? Sounds like Mr. Eha. If he's up all night haunting a hotel, he has to get his rest some time." He said to the woman: "Upstairs, is he? I'll go right up."

"Well," she said doubtfully, "if he sent for you . . . ," and turned away.

One door in the upper hall was closed; Freddy rapped lightly and then walked in. The window shades were down. Mr. Anderson was lying on the bed, fully dressed, but he wasn't asleep, and he turned a scowling red face towards the intruder, and then sat up.

"Hey, who are you? How'd you get in here?"

"I'm Dr. Hopper," said Freddy. "Now, take it easy; I came as soon as I could get here. Ha, you do look bad! But don't worry; we'll have you on your feet in a week or two, or my name's not Henry Hopper." He put his bag down on the table.

Mr. Anderson swung his feet off the bed. "Are you crazy?" he shouted. "I'm not sick, I didn't send for you. Get out! Get out!"

"Stick the tongue out a little farther, please," said Freddy, peering into the man's mouth as he roared at him. "Ha, thought so! Acute frustration of the gulper, with flushed face, bloodshot eyes . . ."

"My eyes are not bloodshot!" roared Mr. Anderson. "Stop talking nonsense and get out of my room. I didn't send for a doctor. There's nothing the matter with me."

Freddy stood back. "Ha! Certainly I'll go," he said in an offended tone. "Never treat a patient against his will. But let me tell you, sir, you're a very sick man. Whether you think so or not, whether you sent for me or not, you're a *ve-ry* sick man! See here, sir; can you honestly tell me that you haven't any pain in the legs, any backache, any soreness in the joints?"

Freddy knew that if this was Mr. Eha, he would certainly be pretty lame from the wrestling match he had had with Mr. Camphor and

Bannister. And he saw that his words had hit the mark. Mr. Anderson frowned and said more quietly: "Well . . . I've got some soreness in my shoulders and my left hip. But it's nothing but . . ."

"Nothing but! Nothing but!" Freddy interrupted. "My dear sir, it's nothing but a severe strain of the spigrastrium, with perhaps a misplacement of the rostrum! Due to some too severe physical exercise. Seen the same thing hundreds of times, and if it isn't taken care of, it always ends badly, badly. Why, look at the back of your hand—complications setting in already!"

"Pooh, that's nothing but a touch of poison ivy," said Mr. Anderson.

"Poison ivy, hey? H'mph, well, it's your funeral." He picked up his bag.

"Just a minute," said the other. He got up and looked at himself in the glass. "Maybe I do look a little flushed. Well, as long as you're here, it won't do any harm if you look me over."

"That's better," said Freddy, putting the bag down again. "Just take off your coat and lie down on the bed. On your face. That's it." He took the coat and as he hung it over the back of a chair, felt in the upper outside pocket. Yes, there were the mothballs. Well, the thing now was to get out as quickly as possible.

He bent over Mr. Anderson and poked at his back, saying: "H'm. Ha. Just as I thought."

"You don't really think anything is wrong, do you, Doctor?" said Mr. Anderson.

"Nothing that a change of climate won't cure," Freddy said. "I'll write you out a prescription." He picked up a pencil at the desk and began making squiggles and curlicues on a piece of paper.

"A change of climate!" Mr. Anderson exclaimed. "I can't leave Centerboro. My business . . ."

"Your business is your affair," Freddy interrupted. "Your health is mine. And I'm telling you that you've got to get away. Another month in this climate and you're a gone goose. Want to spend the rest of your life in a wheel chair? All right. Take six months at the seashore. Then come see me again." He held out the slip of paper on which he had been writing. "Have this filled and take one after every meal until you feel better. Good afternoon, sir."

Mr. Anderson had put on his coat. "Hold

on," he said, looking at the paper. "I can't read this."

"Nobody asked you to," said Freddy. "Let the druggist worry about that. If he can't read it, he'll guess at it. He's pretty good at that. Never killed but one of my patients that way, and that one was no loss."

"Say," Mr. Anderson said, "don't you ever take that hat off?"

"Certainly not. Too busy to waste time. Taking off hats, putting on hats, wastes minutes; minutes add up to hours; I get a week's extra work in the year by keeping this hat on."

Mr. Anderson grinned unpleasantly. "Just the same," he said, "I'd like to see what you look like." And he snatched off the hat. "Great Jerusha!" he exclaimed. "A pig!" And he made a grab for Freddy.

Georgie had curled up under the bush in the yard and was sleeping, as dogs often do, with his eyes open. Suddenly he raised his head. He heard a roaring voice inside the house, and then a great banging and thumping as if a piano was falling downstairs. And then Freddy, hatless, and clutching his medicine case, burst out of the front door and tumbled down the steps, and behind him came Mr. Anderson, shouting: "Stop him! Stop that man—I mean that pig!"

Mr. Anderson's big red hand with the poison ivy on the back was not two inches from Freddy's coat collar. And then Georgie darted out from his bush and dove between his legs.

Mr. Anderson didn't fall at once. But his feet had been stopped by Georgie's body; they had fallen behind his own body which went right on and got ahead of his legs, and though his legs worked hard to catch up and get under him again, they couldn't make it. He took four more steps and then dove headlong into the fence, knocking out four pickets.

"I got him that time!" Georgie yelled. "Beat it, Freddy!"

Freddy was a good runner. But Mr. Anderson was a tough customer; he didn't stop to feel of his bruises; he was up and after the pig in a matter of seconds. They dashed down Clinton into Elm, and down Elm into Main Street. Freddy had only half a block lead, and he knew he could keep it; but his pursuer was yelling: "Stop thief!" at the top of his lungs, and he felt pretty sure that before he got through town somebody would grab and hold him. He turned

Freddy, clutching his medicine case, burst out the front door.

a corner on two legs and darted into the open door of Beller & Rohr's store.

Mr. Rohr was alone in the place. "Hide me!" Freddy panted, and ran into the back room.

Mr. Rohr was a good friend of Freddy's. He didn't ask any questions—indeed, there was hardly time, for a few seconds later Mr. Anderson rushed in.

"Is there a pig in here?" he demanded.

"We don't carry pigs, sir," said Mr. Rohr politely. "This is a jewelry store."

"Certainly I know that, Rohr, you fool," said Mr. Anderson. "I'm looking for a pig in a dark suit that just ran in here—at least he ran into one of these stores."

Mr. Rohr shook his head and smiled faintly. "Pigs in dark suits—if I had seen anything like that, forgive me, Mr. Anderson, but I think I would consult a doctor instead of a jeweler."

"Bah!" said Mr. Anderson disgustedly. "You know the pig I mean, all right. One of those smart animals of old Bean's—I recognized him. Claims to be a detective." He stopped, looking startled. "A detective! By George, I wonder!" He turned and went quickly out of the store.

"Thanks, Mr. Rohr," said Freddy, coming out of the back room. "I'll tell you what it's all about later—can't stop now. Got to find Bannister and get back to Mr. Camphor's. But . . ." He broke off as a loud angry voice began shouting somewhere outside.

Before they could run to the door Georgie came prancing in. "Got him again, Freddy," he said happily. "He pretty near busted the lamp post in front of the bank—dove right into it. I guess I'm even with Mr. Edward Henry Anderson now!"

"Oh, my goodness gracious!" Freddy exclaimed. "Edward Henry Anderson! On that handkerchief—those were his initials: E.H.A.! Mr. Eha! And look at all the work I've done to find out who Mr. Eha was, and there it was right in front of my nose all the time!" Freddy felt pretty angry at himself for being so stupid. But that's the way detective work is—you pass over things forty times without really seeing them at all, and then all at once they seem to jump right up and hit you in the eye. And you wonder how you could have missed them.

Chapter 13

Freddy didn't go straight back to Mr. Camphor's. Instead he went down to call on his friend the sheriff, at the Centerboro jail. The prisoners were all in their cells, getting dressed to go over to a dance that evening at Tushville, and the sheriff took Freddy and Georgie and Bannister into his office and opened a big box of candy, and they sat and munched while Freddy told his story.

The sheriff tugged thoughtfully at his long mustache. "I dunno, Freddy," he said. "I'm sorry for that Mrs. Filmore; she's a real nice woman. And I don't like Anderson—never did. But we haven't got enough against him to do anything legal. Of course, if you got something illegal in your mind, I might help you, as long as you don't tell me what it is. I'm an officer of the law, you know; it wouldn't look right if I was to go round committin' crimes."

"Well, they couldn't put you in jail," said Georgie, "because you're there already."

"That's as true as you're born," said the sheriff with a grin. "But they could take me out of jail, by not electing me next year, and that would be worse."

"I don't want to do anything illegal," Freddy said. "Not now, anyway. All I want is to find out where Simon is. I want to have a talk with him."

"Why the rats could be most anywhere," said the sheriff. "Hold on, though—you say you think Anderson picks 'em up every night and takes 'em over to Lakeside in a canoe? There's a lot of little camps along the south shore of the lake, east of Camphor's; it might be any one of 'em. They're all vacant this time of year."

"Is there any place along there where there's a lot of poison ivy?" Freddy asked.

"There's little patches of it all along that shore. Say, hold on a minute! There's one camp —used to belong to Herb Garble. Come to think of it, Garble bought it off Anderson, seven-eight years ago, but there was so much ivy round the place he couldn't use it much. He was broke out all summer. Place is abandoned now—nobody ever goes there any more. That's the spot I'd pick for a hideaway if I didn't mind doin' a lot of scratching."

"Why don't I drive you up there now?" said Bannister. "He won't be there in the daytime."

"Guess I'll come along," said the sheriff. "I feel kind of out of sorts, seein' the boys all primping and prettying themselves up for the party. Kind of lonesome bein' left here."

"Then why don't you go?" Georgie asked.

"There's two reasons. For one thing I'd have to wear a necktie, and it kind of shuts off my gullet so I ain't got any conversation. For another, my kind of dancin' is the old-fashioned kind—stompin' and yellin' and cuttin' pigeon wings, and folks don't seem to care for it any more. Gone out of style, I guess, like plug hats and red suspenders."

Bannister drove them up to the lake, and then along the southern shore. They passed several camps and cottages, and came to an open space which was covered with the shiny, dark green leaves of poison ivy. In the middle of the space was a tumbledown camp, and the ivy even twined up around the porch posts, and hung in festoons over the boarded-up windows. It didn't look as if anybody had been there in a long time, but Freddy noticed that the path from the road up to the front door had been kept clear. He and Georgie got out, leaving the two men in the car, and walked up to the porch.

"Somebody's been here not later than yesterday," said Freddy, pointing to a leaf on the path, which was crushed, as if somebody had stepped on it, but still green and unwithered.

The flimsy door was padlocked, but Freddy put his shoulder to it and broke it in. There were two rooms. There was nothing in the front one but some odds and ends of furniture, but when they pushed open the door to the kitchen: "Golly!" said Georgie. "This is a regular rat heaven!"

Sacks of grain were stacked in one corner; several were torn open and the grain was spilled out on the floor. A half-eaten cheese was on the table, and there were piles of torn up rags along the walls. Everything was pretty dirty.

Freddy stood in the middle of the floor and called: "Hey, Simon!"

There was no answer.

"Hey, Simon!" he called again. "Do you want to get Ezra back? Mr. Eha hasn't got him any more; I've got him. I want to make a deal with you."

A grey shadow moved in the darkness of one of the holes that had been gnawed in the baseboard, and then a sharp, grey-whiskered nose and two beady black eyes poked out. "Well, well, *well,*" squeaked the rat, "as I live and breathe, if it isn't my old guide and mentor, Freddy the snoop! Welcome, snoop, to rats' castle. And how can we serve you?"

"Serve him with sage and plenty of apple-sauce," came a voice from beneath the floor, and there were loud snickers and another voice said: "Applesauce is right; he's the boy can hand it out. Let's have it, Freddy."

"Look, Simon," Freddy said; "we know all about you and Mr. Eha. We know he's promised you the Bean barn to live in. That's one reason you're working for him. But there's another reason: he's locked up your son, Ezra, and unless you do what he wants you to, you won't get Ezra back. Not all in one piece, anyway.

"A cat! A cruel, clawing cat!" Simon groaned.

But things have changed since last night. We're the ones that have got Ezra now. So I think it may be to your advantage to hear my proposition."

There was a lot more snickering and giggling under the floor, and a voice said: "OK, pig, now tell us the story of the three bears."

"Shut up down there!" Simon snarled.

Then he came out on to the floor. He sat up and drooped his head and folded his forepaws over his stomach and said humbly: "Freddy, those are words to gladden a father's heart. To know that my son, my eldest born, is safe in the care of kindly friends—ah, that is the best news that these old ears have heard in many a day. And where is my boy? Is he well? Forgive a father's anxiety, but the thought of my own son, imprisoned, alone, despairing . . ." He wiped away an imaginary tear.

"He isn't alone," said Freddy. "Jinx is with him."

"A cat! A cruel, clawing cat!" Simon groaned. "But you have promised me that you would release him, that I may again clasp him to my bosom . . ."

"I'll release him when you've carried out my orders," Freddy said. "Any bosom-clasping will have to wait a while, I'm afraid. Listen, Simon. First I want you to tell me everything you know about Mr. Eha."

Simon grinned slyly. "Oh, you know Mr. Eha? Charming fellow, isn't he? One of the oldest families in Philadelphia, the Ehas. But I daresay you know him much better than I. We've merely met casually, at the club and so on."

"Look, rat," said Freddy sternly; "if you're not going to play ball with us, say so right out and we'll know what to do. I'll just point out that Mr. Eha hasn't any hold over you any more because he hasn't got Ezra. We're the ones that have got him. And if you ever want to see him again you'd better do what we ask you to."

"Your threats do not move me," said Simon, striking a noble pose. "It is true that as a father, the thought of my son's peril fills me with consternation. But though I am a father, I am first an animal of honor. How could I ever face the world if, simply to save my son, I were basely to betray a trusting associate? I respect you deeply, I have indeed for you a warm personal regard . . ."

"Just omit the flowers," Freddy interrupted, "and answer yes or no."

"I profoundly regret that my answer must be no," said Simon.

"OK," said Freddy. "I'll just give you a warning. We know your plans. We know you're starting on the Camphor place next, and we're all there, ready and waiting for you. The animals all came up from the farm today, and Mr. Bean came with them. So watch yourself, rat." He turned, and with a jerk of his head to Georgie, left the kitchen. Behind him the giggling broke out again, and some of the rats began singing the old song they had made up about Freddy several years ago:

Freddy the snoop,
The silly old droop,
We'll cut him in pieces and boil him for soup!

Freddy the sneak,
We'll catch him next week,
And after we've caught him, oh boy, how he'll
    squeak!

"My goodness," said Georgie as they went down the path, "he doesn't care much about Ezra."

"He knows we won't do anything very bad to him," Freddy said. "And he still figures that Eha is going to win out."

"And I'm afraid he is going to win out, Freddy," said Mr. Camphor, when they had got back and were sitting on the terrace with him. "Mrs. Filmore just called up and told me that Mr. Anderson had sold Lakeside for her. Sold it for five thousand—about a tenth of what it cost her. Here, have some fudge." He passed them a heaping plate of candy. "I suppose they'll start haunting this house now."

"I don't think you ought to have told them that Mr. Bean and all the animals are up here, Freddy," said Georgie. "We could have ambushed them if you hadn't said that."

"But I told Simon that on purpose," Freddy said. "We can ambush them all right. Don't you see?—they'll tell Eha, and of course Eha will think the Bean farm is going to be unprotected tonight, and my hunch is that he'll change his plans and attack there first. He'll think Mrs. Bean is all alone, and he can tear things up and scare her into fits. And that's a better place to fight him than here: we'll be playing on our home grounds."

"That was right smart of you, Freddy," said the sheriff, who had come along with them. "Say, this fudge is the cat's eyeballs. You make it yourself, Mr. Camphor?"

"My Aunt Minerva made it."

"Oh, are you sure, sir?" said Bannister. "It's not burned."

"The proof of the pudding is in the eating— as you said a while ago, Bannister. And I'll give you another proverb: Two heads are better than one." Mr. Camphor smiled. "Come on, I'll show you the two heads."

He got up and they followed him around the corner of the house to the kitchen window. They looked in. Miss Minerva was at the table, stirring something in a bowl, and Mr. Bean, in a flowered apron, stood at the stove. He had a spice box in one hand and with the other was stirring a kettle of soup. He dipped the spoon and tasted. "Prime!" he said. "What do you think, ma'am—just a dash more celery salt?"

Miss Minerva got up and took the spoon and tasted. "No," she said. "No. One more bay leaf, I think, though." She dropped a bay leaf in, and they stirred and tasted.

"Ma'am," said Mr. Bean, " 'tain't more'n a couple hours since I had my dinner, but I could sit down and eat that whole kettle. You're the champeen cook of the Western Hemisphere!"

"Oh, Mr. Bean!" said Miss Minerva with a simper.

"They've been in there swopping recipes all afternoon," Mr. Camphor whispered. "Funny thing is, all his praising her seems to make the stuff come out better. That fudge was first class."

Freddy took his notebook and went off by himself and sat down on the lawn not far from Miss Elmira's wheel chair. He had a lot of thinking to do. The notebook was indexed, and under A, for convenience in filing he had written: "Aunts, how to get rid of." He looked at the heading for a while and made a note or two. Then he turned to B, and made another heading: "Bean farm, how to protect."

But to protect the farm from Mr. Eha would take a conference of all the animals. They could plan it out when they were walking home after supper—because they would have to leave Mr. Camphor's before dark. So Freddy turned over to P: "Poem, gloomy (for Miss E.)." "Goodness, I feel gloomy enough," he thought; "I ought to be able to write something pretty dismal." He licked his pencil and went to work.

Miss Elmira didn't look at Freddy when he sat down in the grass beside her wheel chair half an hour later. She just stared off across the lake, and you would have thought by her expression that instead of gay sparkling blue water she was seeing black clouds and tornadoes and thunder and lightning.

He didn't begin reading his poem to her right off. He gave a couple of deep groans, followed by a sob or two, and then in a low voice, interrupted by very damp sniffs, he began to recite:

> *"Look on me, mournfulest of pigs!*
> *Ye birds, sit silent on your twigs;*
> *Sing not to me of joy and glee, restrain your*
> *merry carols!*
> *My eyes are dim, my nose is red,*
> *Because of all the tears I've shed—*
> *And I shall keep on shedding them, in pints*
> *and quarts and barrels.*

> *"I care not for these sunny hills,*
> *This garden, bright with laughing rills;*
> *Grim desert wastes best suit my tastes, or cel-*
> *lars, damp and dismal.*
> *I like to sob, I love to weep.*
> *I even snivel in my sleep,*
> *And when I wake, make no mistake, my grief*
> *is still abysmal."*

At this point Freddy stopped reciting and appeared to break down completely. He buried his face in his handkerchief, and his shoulders shook.

"More," said Miss Elmira.

Freddy looked up at her, wiping the tears from his eyes. And they were real tears all right, because if you pretend to cry hard enough, pretty soon you get to crying in real earnest. You probably know this as well as I do.

Miss Elmira was looking much less gloomy; her eyes were bright, and the corners of her mouth had taken a slight upward curve. "More, more!" she said, and pounded the arm of her chair with her hand.

So Freddy went on:

> *"And so I sit upon this shore*
> *And weep and moan and howl and roar*
> *Because I hate to contemplate a scene so bright*
>   *and cheery.*
> *I'll turn my back on joy and pomp*
> *And seek me out a deep dark swamp*
> *Where all the sights are blots and blights, and*
>   *all the sounds are dreary.*
>
> *"And there within that quaking bog,*
> *Enveloped in unwholesome fog,*
> *Alone I'll sit, enjoying it, while black bats flit*
>   *and tumble;*

There'll be no sound except the plop
Of steady tears that drip and drop
From off my nose into the ooze where alligators
    grumble.

"I'd rather be within that swamp
Than out where children play and romp;
I hear the bullfrogs calling me, the marsh fires
    gleam and beckon.
Oh, there I'll go—yes, there I'll go,
Where I can fill my soul with woe.
No more I'll roam, for my true home is in a
    swamp, I reckon."

Freddy stopped again. Miss Elmira was smiling. She put her hand up and fingered her mouth, as if she wanted to feel what a smile was like. She took a little mirror out of her bag and looked in it. "Beautiful!" she said, and Freddy didn't know whether she meant the smile or the poem. Then she said: "More!"

"I'm sorry," he said; "there isn't any more. Except a sort of chorus. If only I had my guitar, I could sing it to you." He began to cry again. "But I c-can't play the guitar!" he sobbed.

"Sing away," she commanded.

He sang:

"So I weep (sniff, sniff),
So I cry and sob and moan.
In the deep (sniff, sniff)
Dark swamp I'll be alone."

Freddy said afterwards that the sniffs, which were exceedingly damp and realistic, were what really got Miss Elmira. For she laughed right out, a thin high cackle, that appeared to surprise her even more than it did Freddy. "Sing some more!" she said. "I want to hear some more."

"That's all I've written so far," said Freddy. "Perhaps tonight I'll feel worse, and I'll write another one for you."

"Hey, Freddy!" someone called from the house. He got up and excused himself.

Miss Elmira held out her hand. "Thank you," she said. "Thank you very much."

Freddy bowed over her hand, and managed to drop a tear on it. "I'll write some more for you," he said.

Bannister came to meet him. "We're serving a picnic supper, sir—on the terrace. Because of the large number of guests."

"What is it tonight, Bannister?" Freddy

asked. "Singed soufflé? Burnt broth? Scorched succotash? Cinder stew?"

"You're very merry, sir," said the butler. "I find that is always the effect of sitting a while with Miss Elmira. But you'll be surprised. Your Mr. Bean has worked wonders with the cooking—just by laying out a few compliments. The supper is excellent."

And it was excellent. Mr. Camphor sat at the head of a long table on the terrace with Mrs. Wiggins on his right, and Miss Minerva sat at the foot, with Mr. Bean beside her. The animals were seated along the sides. Bannister served dish after dish, and from the soup right through to the apple pie not a dish was even lightly scorched. Miss Minerva chatted gaily with Mr. Bean, and acknowledged with a pleasant smile the many compliments that Mr. Camphor and the animals showered upon her cooking. "I've never seen such a change in anybody in my life," Freddy murmured to Mr. Camphor.

"I guess Mrs. Wiggins had the right of it," Mr. Camphor replied. "And your Mr. Bean showed the way with his compliments. I never praised her in my life, now I come to think of it. I was always too scared of her."

"Well," said Freddy, "it doesn't cost much to pass out a few words of praise. And it sure gets results. If Miss Minerva gets kind of mellowed down, maybe you won't be so anxious to have her go."

After supper Charles got up and made a speech, thanking Mr. Camphor for his hospitality, and thanking particularly Miss Minerva for what he called "Her display of supreme culinary skill. As an artist," he said, "in the field of food, she ranks among the great names of all time. For such a dinner as we tonight have had the privilege of adding to the memories of great meals of the past, can only be considered a high work of art. Not Rembrandt, not Shakespeare, not Beethoven, have ever risen to such heights. And we pay tribute to her, not only as artist, but as a great lady. In that field too she reigns supreme. Before her, queens bow the knee, empresses topple from their thrones, duchesses and countesses fall flat on their faces. The brightest stars in the heavens of femininity go pop and expire. Ladies and gentlemen, animals, birds and insects (if any), I call for three cheers for that fairest flower of the Camphor clan, that pearl beyond price, Miss Minerva Camphor!"

I don't suppose anybody had ever before given even one feeble cheer for Miss Minerva, and when the animals all got up and shouted, first she blushed, and then she broke right down and cried.

Then Mr. Bean got up. "I ain't any great shakes as a speaker," he said. "I just want to say that I agree—lock, stock and barrel; hook, line and sinker; top, sides and middle—with every word of the last speaker, even though I didn't understand 'em all. And I call for three more cheers for all the Camphors, whomsoever and wheresoever they may be, whether among those present, or elsewhere and otherwise. And I want to add that if Mrs. B. was here she'd cheer louder than any of you."

Then when the cheers had been given, he said: "I don't like to eat and run, but from all I hear, maybe that Eha figures on payin' me a call tonight, and I want to heat up a little something for him. So, you animals: we leave in ten minutes. Mr. Camphor, sir, we'll be back, when and if you need us. And between us, if we can't pull Eha's fangs for him we ain't the man I think we are."

Chapter 14

At ten o'clock that night, the hastily formed Committee for Animal Defence had put the Bean farm in a state of siege. Mr. Bean was on guard inside the house with his shotgun, ready to rush at a second's notice to any threatened quarter. The smaller animals, and those of the birds who could be trusted to stay awake after dark, were patrolling the farm's boundaries, with instructions to give warning if the enemy was sighted, but to let them through and not put up any resistance. Freddy and Mrs. Wiggins, who headed the Committee as chairman and chairwoman respectively, had set up field headquarters in the cowbarn, which had doors on all four sides, so that animals could enter or leave it without being observed by the enemy. The other animals occupied various strategic posts.

The animals figured that the attack, when it came, would be double: by the rats, to destroy as much property as possible, and an attempt by Mr. Eha to scare the living daylights out of Mrs. Bean, whom he supposed to be alone in the house. And so the window shades in the parlor, which were usually pulled down to keep the afternoon sun from fading the carpet, had been raised, and all the lights turned on; and Mrs. Bean sat at the table, darning socks. At least she looked from the outside as if she was darning socks, but actually it was so long after her usual nine o'clock bedtime that she had gone sound asleep.

Several years earlier when the animals had made their famous attack on the Grimby house in the Big Woods, they had been organized into an army, and the organization had been kept up. The birds formed the air arm; the scouts were the rabbits and other small animals; the goat, Bill, the cows, and Hank were the shock troops; and a separate division was formed of all those who had teeth and claws to fight with —Freddy, Jinx, the dogs, Peter, the bear, and his relatives, and John, the fox. Jacob, the wasp, and his family were attached to the air arm as dive bombers, and there was even a chemical warfare division, armed with fire extinguishers and pepper shakers, and a garden sprayer which they had filled with several bottles of household ammonia.

All in all, a much more formidable garrison than Simon and Mr. Eha, even if they had not supposed the farm unprotected, could have expected to attack. And as it grew later, more volunteers came trickling in from the woods and fields in answer to the appeal for help that Freddy had sent out by rabbit. Sniffy Wilson, the skunk, and his family came, and were attached to the chemical warfare division. Cecil, the porcupine, came, his quills rattling as he walked, and Uncle Solomon, the little screech owl, and even several animals from the Schemerhorn farm.

It was nearly eleven o'clock when a rabbit came bounding into the cowbarn to announce that a car had stopped just below the First Animal Bank, which was a shed a couple of hundred yards down the Centerboro road. A tall man had got out, had climbed the fence, and, followed by a big gang of rats, was coming towards the barnyard across the fields.

"OK," said Freddy. "Now keep quiet, everybody. We mustn't let 'em think there's anybody here but Mrs. Bean. Uncle Solomon, suppose you could fly out and keep track of where the rats go?"

"Very well," said the owl in his precise little voice. "I am supposing it."

"Oh, come on, come on!" said Freddy. "There isn't time to argue about the way I use words. Go on, do it, will you?"

"Observe, Freddy," Uncle Solomon said; "if I tell you to suppose a thing, I am not asking you to do it; I am merely ordering you to imagine that you *can* do it. If you want me actually to do it, why didn't you say so in the first place?"

Jinx growled at him. "Look, owl," he said; "suppose I give you a good smack in the beak?"

Uncle Solomon gave his little crazy laugh. "It is not a supposition that appeals to me," he said, and spreading his wings, flew out of the door.

"I don't know," said Jinx; "sometimes I wonder how I keep my claws out of that fel-

low's tailfeathers, the way he picks at everything you say."

"He doesn't mean anything by it," said Freddy. "It's kind of fun, sometimes at that. Only
not right now. Quiet, everybody. Not a sound
till you get the signal."

The animals stood in the door, silently
watching. Nothing happened for a minute or
two, then Uncle Solomon came floating in
through the doorway and lit on Mrs. Wiggins'
shoulder. "He's up behind the fence, getting
into his ghost costume," he whispered. "The
rats will be along in a minute; he told 'em to
go into the stable and get to work."

Almost immediately there was a rustling and
pattering of small feet as the rats, invisible in
the darkness, swept by the cowbarn. Then a
white figure appeared on the other side of the
barnyard, and walked slowly towards the house.

Georgie began to giggle. "He looks so darn
silly!" he whispered. "Can't I trip him up
again, Freddy?"

"Oh, be still," Freddy murmured. "You've
had your fun with him; let Mr. and Mrs. Bean
have theirs."

Mr. Eha went up to the lighted window.
Tap, tap, tap, tap! he rapped on the pane.

But Mrs. Bean didn't look up. Her head was bent, her eyes were closed, and her spectacles had slipped down to the end of her nose. "Oh, dear!" Freddy thought. "She wanted so much to see the ghost, and she's gone to sleep!"

Mr. Eha took something from under the sheet and reached up to the window. Rap, rap, *crash!* He broke the pane.

Mrs. Bean's head jerked up and she opened her eyes with a start. She looked vaguely around the room but didn't seem to notice the window. "M'm," she said. "Must have dropped off." She gathered up her darning. "Lands sakes, it's after eleven!"

Mr. Eha drew a deep breath and let out a long hideous screech. Then he dropped down against the house, out of sight of the window.

Mrs. Bean didn't appear startled. She got up and raised the window sash without appearing to see the broken pane, although the glass scrunched under her feet. "Those pesky owls!" she said as she leaned out. "Make such a racket a body can't get a minute's quiet!"

Then Mr. Eha stood up suddenly, so that the cat mask with its ferocious grin was within an inch of her face. "Yaaaaaah!" he yelled.

Mrs. Bean never batted an eyelash. "Dear me

suz!" she said. "Where in tunket did you come from?"

Mr. Eha seemed taken aback. He hesitated a moment, then he said in a slow hollow voice: "I come from beyond the tomb."

"Oh," she said, "guess you're one of the Gurney boys from over beyond the cemetery. Well, where's your manners, young man? If you want something, why don't you come to the front door like a sensible human being?"

"I am no human," he said. "I am a spirit—a messenger from the underworld."

"Oh, you're a ghost," said Mrs. Bean. "Always seemed like a lonely sort of occupation to me—flitting about wailing in empty houses. Not that the houses are always empty. This one, for instance—it's been haunted for years. The ghost of Mr. Bean's grandfather—Bezaliel Bean. Won't you come in and meet him? Come around to the front door—unless of course you prefer to seep through the keyhole."

Mr. Eha hesitated again. Evidently his failure to frighten Mrs. Bean had puzzled him, but he knew she was alone in the house, and he must have thought that if he went in, he would be able to think up something more terrifying. "I will enter," he said. "Turn the lamp out."

From the door of the cowbarn the animals had heard every word. Then as Mr. Eha started around to the front door, Freddy said: "Come on, we can't miss this. The rats will be busy for some time; we can attend to them later." So they all crept out and crouched together under the broken window.

They heard the parlor door creak, and Mrs. Bean say: "Don't like much light, you say? Bezaliel doesn't either. I've turned the lamp down a ways. Sit down over there. It's pretty late, but I'm not a mite sleepy, and we can have a good talk. Now just who did you say you were?"

"Woman," said the ghost, raising his voice so it boomed through the house, "let us have no more of this silly chatter. I come to warn you. This house is doomed! Doomed, as are those who dwell in it. Tremble—and depart from it while there is yet time."

"Dear me," said Mrs. Bean, "you seem very depressed." She smiled at him. "You do remind me a lot of Bezaliel—he always talks like that. Let's see if he can't cheer you up." She raised her voice. "Bezaliel, are you there?"

There were three heavy knocks on the ceiling.

Freddy had got his eyes up over the level of the windowsill. He saw Mr. Eha give a start, and half rise.

"Grandfather is a little shy with strangers," said Mrs. Bean. She got up and opened the door into the front hall. "Come down, Bezaliel," she called. "You've got company."

There was silence for a minute, then a deep groaning voice somewhere in the darkness of the upper hall said: "I come!"

And then Freddy himself got a real scare. The parlor door was a black oblong, through which he could just dimly make out the shapes of the front stairs banisters. And in front of the banisters something vaguely white fluttered and danced a spectral dance—and groaned again: "I come!"

That finished Mr. Eha. He gave a very unghostly yell and leaped up and dove straight through the window—and landed scrunch on top of Cecil, the porcupine, knocking the wind out of him. It was in a way unfortunate that he fell on Cecil. If he had landed on one of the other animals there would have been a second or two before he could get to his feet, and they might have taken him prisoner. But he rebounded from Cecil as a man rebounds from a chair seat on which a tack has been placed. For Cecil was worse than a whole box of tacks; dozens of his sharp, barbed quills were driven into Mr. Eha's stomach, and the pain lifted him from the ground and fairly shot him off across the barnyard before the animals could grab him.

Things happened very quickly after that. "Don't chase him!" Freddy shouted. "He's got a gun. Peter, Bill, and the cows—cut across lots down to the bank; you can beat him to his car. The rest of us to the barn!"

Boom! went Mr. Bean's shotgun from an upper window, and then boom! from the second barrel, and at the second boom Mr. Eha, just climbing the fence, gave another yell and leaped in the air. But he kept on going.

Freddy and the others had already surrounded the barn, which squeaked and rustled excitedly. There was a scrabbling on the roof, and a rat dropped from the eaves and scurried off in the long grass before anybody could seize him.

"You're surrounded, Simon," Freddy called. "Come out, one by one."

Nobody answered. There was a fluttering and a thin shriek from the roof, and Uncle

He landed scrunch on top of Cecil, the porcupine.

Solomon's neat little laugh floated down to them. "Would anyone else like his whiskers trimmed?"

"Last call, Simon," said Freddy.

This time Simon answered. "Come in and get us, you big lopsided fat snoop!"

"Tut, tut, such language!" said Freddy. "OK, Robert, try the sprayer."

So Robert dragged the sprayer up to the door and stuck the nozzle inside and squeezed the trigger. The ammonia did the trick. There was a great outburst of sneezing and coughing and wheezing in the stable, and then the rats charged out. Luckily for them, Sniffy Wilson and his family had been set to guard one or two weak places in the side walls, where Freddy had felt that they might be able to break out. So there were in front of them only Jinx and Freddy and John and the two dogs, with a dozen or more woodchucks and squirrels.

There were probably twenty rats in the gang, and rats are wicked fighters, especially in the dark. But at that moment Mr. Bean came out of the kitchen door and snapped on the big porch light, so that the barnyard was almost as bright as day. There was a sprawl of snapping and snarling in front of the stable door as the animals leaped and slashed and clawed and bit. Freddy spied Simon, and with a lucky snap of his jaws caught him by the back of the neck, but was immediately attacked from behind by two other rats, who climbed up on his shoulders and bit savagely. He squealed and reared up and fell over backward on them, but he had dropped Simon, who slipped away. The rats he had fallen on, however, were out cold.

Freddy looked around for another enemy, but the rats, half strangled by the ammonia fumes, were more anxious to escape than to fight, and except for half a dozen who had been knocked out or captured, were in full retreat. Freddy saw them scattering for cover, but he was too winded to give chase. He saw Simon galloping along in the lead, and as he looked, the old rat climbed up on a fence post. "We'll be back, pig!" he squeaked defiantly.

And then . . .

Boom! went Mr. Bean's shotgun. And Simon toppled and slid slowly to the ground.

There was a minute's silence.

"You know," said Freddy, "I'm kind of sorry to see that. Old Simon!"

"He was a liar and a sneak, and he got what was coming to him," said Jinx shortly.

"Maybe. But he wasn't a coward. That's more than you can say for most crooks.—Hey, what's that?" A faint cry for help had come to them.

They went over to the fence. Simon lay on his side in the grass. He opened one eye. "Tell old Bean," he murmured, "to load with buckshot next time. You can't kill a rat with that little stuff." Then he closed his eyes again.

It was Jinx who picked him up and carried him carefully into the cowbarn, where he was laid out beside the other casualties of the fight. Mrs. Bean came out with iodine and bandages and a large bottle of cod liver oil, which was her favorite remedy for everything from nosebleed to measles, and she dabbed and bound and dosed the animals until as Georgie said, gritting his teeth as she put some iodine on a torn ear, it would have been more fun if they'd all been killed.

"Stop talking and open your mouth!" said Mrs. Bean, and popped in a tablespoonful of oil.

Counting the two that Freddy had fallen on, eight rats had been taken prisoner. There had been several teeth knocked out in the fight. One squirrel had lost the end of his tail, and there were any number of bites to be dressed. Cecil of course was badly shaken, and had lost thirty-four quills. And Sniffy Wilson's daughter, Aroma, who had not been in the fight at all, had fainted away from excitement.

But of course Simon was the most seriously wounded. "Hold the candle here, Freddy," said Mrs. Bean. "Good land, he's as full of birdshot as a muffin is of blueberries. We'll have to dig 'em out."

"Leave 'em in, ma'am," said the rat. "They'll bring me up nearer the right fighting weight the next time I tackle that pig."

"We'll dig 'em out," said Mrs. Bean, and went to work at it.

"Ouch!" said Simon. "I guess you enjoy this kind of work."

"I don't enjoy hurting anybody, even a rat," she said. "I'd help anybody that was sick. Except maybe a mosquito," she added thoughtfully.

Bill, Peter and the cows came back presently and said that they'd found Mr. Eha's car down by the bank and had turned it over in the ditch, but had seen nothing of Eha himself. "Smart guy," said Bill. "He knew we'd go down there and probably went home cross country."

"I wish we'd captured him," said Mrs. Wiggins. "I don't suppose we can have him arrested; we haven't a mite of proof that he's really Mr. Anderson."

"We can prove that's his car," said Peter.

"He'll just say somebody stole it and ditched it," Freddy said.

"Come, come," said a gruff voice and there was Mr. Bean in the doorway. "Time you animals were in bed. Mrs. B., if you've got 'em fixed up, you'd better be seekin' your downy couch yourself."

The animals grinned happily at him, for they knew that when he used such flowery language he was in pretty high spirits.

"Well, Mr. B.," Mrs. Bean replied, "seems to me you could say a word of thanks to your animals. After the brave fight they put up to keep a roof over our heads."

"Roof's over their heads too, ain't it?" he said. Then he stood up straight and thought and thought, and cleared his throat about fifteen times, and at last he said: "Animals!" After that he didn't say anything more for quite a long time, but finally he did make a sort of speech.

"Animals," he said, "you don't want thanks

and you don't want praise. You did just what I expected of you, and that's the best praise I can give you. Because I guess I expect more of you than Schemerhorn or Witherspoon or Macy or any of these other farmers expect of their animals. Maybe you expect more of me, too. But don't go expectin' a lot of high-class oratory. If that's what you want, go live with Senator Blore, out on the hill t'other side of Centerboro. He's given away free, gratis and for nothing more fancy highfalutin language than any man in the county. But he never gave away anything that cost him more than maybe a sore throat. You folks that look to me, you'll get taken care of without any fuss and feathers, and . . ." He stopped. "There I go, talking politics!" he said. "Well, I'm proud of you . . . that's all I've got to say."

The animals didn't applaud much because they felt that Mr. Bean wouldn't like it. But they all felt very warm inside. And Jinx called out: "How about a word of thanks for Grandfather Bezaliel?"

Mr. Bean stared at the cat a moment, then from behind his whiskers came the fizzing sound that the animals had come to learn was laughter. "So you liked the old rapscallion, did you?" he said. "Well, I guess old Bezaliel has gone back to his home, wherever his home is. But he'll always come back if we need him. Eh, grandfather?" And the groaning voice came from behind the whiskers: "Whenever you say, grandson."

The animals yelled delightedly, but after a minute he held up his hand. "Time to go to bed," he said, and stumped off towards the house.

Mrs. Bean followed after a minute, and Freddy walked across the barnyard with her. "Excuse me, ma'am," he said, "but I just wanted to know how Mr. Bean made that ghost dance out in the hall. It was ten times as scary as Mr. Eha, with all his false faces and yelling."

"Of course it was," said Mrs. Bean. "False faces and yelling make you jump, but a little flutter of white in the darkness, when you know there's nothing there, makes you curl right up inside. It was just a shirt of Mr. Bean's; he tied a string to it and let it down from the upper hall. And we knew Mr. Eha was deathly afraid of ghosts."

"How did you know that?" Freddy asked.

"Why, because he is so sure that everybody else is afraid of them. If you like something, or want something, or are afraid of something yourself, you're pretty apt to think that everybody else in the world likes or wants or is afraid of the same thing. You like poetry, and so you think everybody else does too. Though I expect you've found out by this time that there are some folks that think it's all a lot of foolishness."

"Come along, Mrs. B." said Mr. Bean from the doorway. Then he fumbled in his pocket and held out something in his hand to Freddy. "Some of that fudge," he said. "I brought a little with me, to eat before I went to bed. But I'd like you to have it." Then he whacked Freddy on the back. "Go on, now. Go to bed."

Chapter 15

Freddy was up early next morning. It was a dull drizzly day, and he shivered as he hurried down to the stable to take a look at the prisoners. They were locked up in the box stall next to Hank's, and guarded by Jacob, the wasp, and two of his cousins. Simon was asleep on an old grain bag and breathing heavily, but the others were awake, and they stared at the pig anxiously with their beady black eyes, but didn't say anything.

Jacob flew down and lit on Freddy's nose. "Everything's under control," he said. "Caught one of 'em starting to gnaw through the wall a while back, but I guess he won't do any more gnawing for a while. Had to give him a little touch of the old needle. My, my; such language as he used!

"Tough, he was, too," Jacob went on. "Afraid I blunted my sting on his thick skull." He slid it out and placed the point on the tip of Freddy's snout. "Mind if I just try it a mite here? I won't hurt you."

Freddy thought Jacob was joking, but it was hard to tell, for wasps only have one expression on their faces, and even that one doesn't express anything. "No!" he said. "Lay off, Jacob!" He stared apprehensively at the wasp, and some of the rats began to giggle.

Jacob leaped into the air and droned in a circle above their heads. "None of that!" he buzzed. "You show a proper respect for your betters if you know what's good for you."

"Oh, please, Mr. Jacob," said one of them; "we didn't—we weren't laughing at you. It was Mr. Freddy—he looked cross-eyed at you."

"Why, I did nothing of the kind," said Freddy.

"Oh, excuse me, sir," squealed the rat. "I guess you had to look cross-eyed to see him, because he was on the end of your nose."

"Oh," Freddy said. "Well, maybe I did." He frowned at the rat. "Aren't you the one that bit me last night?"

"Well, sir—I . . ."

"Answer yes or no, please," said Freddy, putting on his Great Detective expression.

"Well, I—yes, I did. But you sat on me, afterwards."

"I see. You mean we're even. Maybe you're right. Although—Oh, good morning, Jinx," he said, as the cat pushed open the stall door.

"Just dropped in to see if the condemned man was eating the usual hearty breakfast," said Jinx. He went over and sat down by Simon. "How's old poisonous this morning?"

Simon opened one eye, then closed it again.

"Let him alone, Jinx," said Freddy. "He's got trouble enough coming to him when he gets well. Come on out; I want to talk to you."

They went out into the barnyard. Charles was just coming across from the henhouse, and Jinx hailed him. "Hi, Charlie, old fighting cock! You certainly put up a great scrap last night. I saw you in there, stomping and goug-

ing and ripping off arms and legs, and I said:
Boy, there's a rooster that could lick his weight
in lollipops, and . . ."

"Oh, shut up!" said Charles crossly. "You
know very well I wasn't there last night. I—
well, with this farm invaded by hordes of ferocious rats, would you have expected me to leave
my home, my dear wife, and twenty-seven children, totally unprotected? Much as I would like
to have been with you, to have stood shoulder
to shoulder with my comrades in the fray, my
duty confined me to the henhouse. Yes, my
friend, the heart that beats beneath this feath-
ered bosom is no craven's; it . . ."

"Boloney!" said Jinx. "It was your dear wife
Henrietta that confined you to the henhouse,
chum, so you wouldn't get those handsome tailfeathers chewed off. Don't give us that shoulder
to shoulder stuff, and you can cut out the feath-
ered bosom, too."

Charles hung his head, and Freddy felt sorry
for him. The rooster was a braggart, and badly
henpecked by his wife, but he wasn't really a
coward. He had once licked a rat in fair fight,
and a year or so ago he had gone into Herb
Garble's office in Centerboro and cleaned it out
singlehanded. "Charles," said Freddy, "how'd

you like to go up to Mr. Camphor's with me to-morrow? We've got to do something about those aunts of his, and maybe you could help."

Charles perked up at once. "Command me," he said magnificently. "It is a pleasure and a privilege to serve Mr. Camphor."

So the next morning they started out. It was still raining, but though animals don't mind rain as much as people do, Freddy carried Mrs. Bean's old plum-colored umbrella. "It won't do to go into Mr. Camphor's spick and span parlor all dripping wet," he said. "And Miss Minerva would have a fit."

"She'll have a fit anyway," said Charles.

"That's up to you," Freddy said. "That's why I wanted you to come. You think up your floweriest compliments for her."

They were pretty wet though when they got there. Bannister brought them bath towels to dry off with before they went into the parlor, and they were scrubbing themselves when Miss Minerva appeared.

"My land!" she exclaimed. "You're dripping all over the rug! Why do you have to come up here on a day like this?"

"Madam," said Charles, "only the anticipation of seeing you again so soon could have in-

Freddy carried Mrs. Bean's old plum-colored umbrella.

duced us to brave the inclemency of the elements."

"Well . . ." said Miss Minerva doubtfully.

"Your gracious presence, ma'am," the rooster went on, "transforms the gloomiest hours to a day of sparkling sunshine and balmy breezes. In the light of your charming smile the clouds disperse, the sun breaks through, the world is all brightness and glitter." He bowed deeply.

And a smile did indeed appear on Miss Minerva's face. It wouldn't have dispersed any clouds, nor could you have recognized it from Charles' description, but it was a smile. "Come into the parlor," she said.

Mr. Camphor had news. The sheriff had phoned to say that Mr. Anderson was sick in bed, but was expected out in a day or two. "Guess he has a hard time getting comfortable, though," the sheriff had said. "Porky quills in front and bird shot in the rear—has to sleep on his side."

"Well, that's nice," said Freddy. "But it isn't really any good. For though we've broken up his scheme for getting your house and the Beans', he has got the hotel."

"Come out on the porch," said Mr. Camphor, and when they had followed him out there: "Listen," he said.

The rain had let up, and from across the lake they could hear a faint sound of hammering.

"Carpenters," said Mr. Camphor. "Plumbers. He's got them repairing the hotel already. According to the sheriff, he is going to move up there himself as soon as he's well enough. It's a shame. But what can we do?"

"I think . . ." Freddy began. But a voice from the end of the porch interrupted him. "Come here," it said. He looked, and there was Miss Elmira in her chair, wrapped in shawls and gazing out gloomily at the grey lake.

He went over to her and Charles strutted after him, but Mr. Camphor disappeared in the house.

"Poem," said Miss Elmira.

"I haven't written any other gloomy ones yet," he said.

"Swamp," said Miss Elmira.

"Oh, you want that one again? All right." And he recited it, with appropriate sobs and sniffs.

Miss Elmira laughed even more heartily than before, but Charles, who had listened with one claw covering his eyes, broke down and wept bitterly. "Oh! Oh, dear! Oh, dear me!" he said brokenly. "Oh, the sadness! Oh, my desolate heart! How mournfully beautiful! What a masterpiece of despair!"

Freddy thought the rooster was overdoing it, and shook his head at him, for Miss Elmira had stopped laughing. She looked almost disapprovingly at Charles. "Always like that?" she demanded.

"Always," said Freddy. "Always wallowing in woe, soaked in sorrow, fricasseed in affliction. Worst case I've ever known."

Charles went on sobbing.

Miss Elmira's shoulders twitched impatiently. Then she said: "Go away."

"Of course," said Freddy. "Come, my poor fellow," and he supported the weeping Charles into the house.

The rooster straightened when they were inside the door. "That was a terrible poem, Freddy," he said. "If I couldn't write a better one with one claw tied behind my back . . ."

"Oh, you're a wonder," said Freddy sarcastically. "You fixed things fine with all that bawling! She knew you were making it up."

"On the contrary," said Charles. "She was

mad, all right, but it was because she had met someone who is gloomier than she is. You've got her all wrong. She doesn't want other people to be gloomy. She wants to be the gloomiest person in the house, herself. What do you suppose she stays here for, if everybody is always trying to cheer her up? She likes it. She wouldn't stay a minute if everybody sobbed and howled all day long."

"Oh, pooh," said Freddy; "that doesn't make sense."

"Yeah, just because *you* didn't think of it!" said Charles angrily. "All right, have it your way. But if Camphor wants to get rid of her, he'd better let me handle it, that's all."

Freddy really thought that maybe Charles was right, but he knew that if he took up the idea himself the rooster would just sit back and not do anything. So he continued to pooh-pooh the theory until Charles got really mad and said that by George, he'd show them, and stamped out of the house.

Chapter 16

Freddy went in and had a long talk with Mr. Camphor, and at his pressing invitation, stayed for lunch. "I really want you to see, Freddy," Mr. Camphor said, "what a change a few compliments have made in Aunt Minerva. Nothing burned, no bawlings out; and she made a batch of peanut brittle last night that—m'm!" He blew a kiss in the air. "It would melt in your mouth!"

So Freddy stayed. A place was set for Charles, but when Bannister announced lunch the rooster couldn't be found, so they sat down without him. When Miss Minerva came in, Freddy pulled out her chair for her, and she rewarded him with a smile. At least it was intended for a smile. She really just showed her teeth at him. But it wasn't fair to be too critical of it, Freddy thought, because probably she hadn't really smiled in a good many years, and she needed practice.

The soufflé was good, the chocolate pie was delicious. "The nectar of the gods!" Mr. Camphor exclaimed with his mouth full, and was not reproved for it. Freddy smacked his lips and said: "M'm! M'mmm!" all through the meal. Miss Minerva became quite sprightly.

"She doesn't pick on me any more either," Mr. Camphor said later. "I used the wrong fork at dinner last night, and she didn't say a word."

"Then do you still want her to go?" Freddy asked.

Mr. Camphor thought a moment. "Really, you know," he said, "I don't believe I do. I haven't eaten so well in years. But of course there's Aunt Elmira. Look at her there through the window. What's the good of having Aunt Minerva cooking for me if Aunt Elmira takes away my appetite?"

"I've got to give some thought to that," said

Freddy. "Also to Mr. Eha. We've broken up the rat gang all right, and I guess he realizes that the ghost act won't get him anywhere. But he did get the hotel away from poor Mrs. Filmore. I think we ought to get it back for her."

Mr. Camphor shook his head. "Nothing can be done about that now. We've got her a job, though. I used my influence with Mr. Weezer, in the bank, and they've taken her on at a small salary."

"That's fine," said Freddy. "But Eha's got the hotel, and I don't see why we can't use the same tactics against him that he did against Mrs. Filmore. Not rats and ghosts, of course— I've got a better idea." He looked thoughtfully at Mr. Camphor. "How'd you like to go camping again?"

"Oh, I'd like that!" said Mr. Camphor enthusiastically. "We didn't have much of a go at it before. Ha, the wide open spaces! The mysterious silence of the great forest! The wind shushing through the pines . . ."

"And the mosquitoes whining through the brush," said Freddy. "Yeah, it's pretty nice. But this will be something more than a camping trip. It'll be an anti-Eha expedition. A war party."

"Ha, Camphor takes the warpath, eh? Let's practice our warwhoop." And he gave a loud yell, batting his open palm against his mouth— "Wa-wa-wa-wa!"

"I don't think the Indian warwhoop went like that," Freddy said. "It was more like this." And then he yelled: "Yi-yi-yi-yi!"

"What on earth are you doing?" said Miss Minerva, coming to the door. She looked at them rather severely, but didn't fly out at them. And when Mr. Camphor had rather shame-facedly explained, she astonished them by saying: "You're both wrong. Grandfather showed me. This is the way it went," and she threw back her head and gave a terrific screech: "Eeeee-yow!"

"Golly," said Mr. Camphor; "you win, Aunt. Say, how'd you like to go along on this expedition? You used to camp out with grandfather, years ago."

"Oh, I don't know," she said. "I—well, I suppose Bannister could look after Elmira . . . H'm . . . Very well," she said quickly. "I'll come."

Freddy wasn't too well pleased with this but there was nothing he could do. After lunch he started back to the farm. The rain had stopped.

Going down through the Big Woods he heard voices, and then Mrs. Wiggins' broad white nose pushed through the underbrush, and she came towards him, followed by her two sisters. Charles was riding on Mrs. Wurzburger's back.

"Where you going?" Freddy asked. "And where'd you go to, Charles? They expected you for lunch."

Mrs. Wiggins laughed. "We're going up to call on Miss Elmira. It's Charles' idea. He thinks if everybody she sees is gloomier than she is, she'll either snap out of it, or leave. And we're good at grief, eh, girls?"

Mrs. Wogus and Mrs. Wurzburger nodded. Then all three cows looked sadly at Freddy, and pulled their mouths down, and fat tears welled out of their big brown mournful eyes and splashed on the ground.

Freddy looked at them a minute, and then he felt the corners of his own mouth droop, and a tightness behind his eyes and a stinging in them, and he said: "Hey, quit it, will you? Darn it, you're m-making me do it, too! I can't . . . Well, goodbye," he said and pushed quickly past them.

He went into the cowbarn and yelled for Mr. Webb, and pretty soon a little black spider

"Hey, quit it, will you . . . you're m-making me do it, too!"

came spinning down on a strand of gossamer and landed on his ear. "Hello, Freddy," he said in his tiny voice. "You know, Mother and I are kind of put out that you haven't called on us for any help in all this excitement. After all, the Bean farm is our home just as much as it is yours."

"Well," said Freddy, "we can use you now all right. Look, can you and Mrs. Webb round up about fifty crickets, and as many fireflies, and some grasshoppers and a centipede or two? Just get those that are willing to volunteer for foreign service; I want their help up at Camphor's, but only if they want to go."

"Round up a bushel of 'em if you say so, Freddy. My! Won't Mother be tickled! She says she's sick and tired of sitting up there in the roof spinning, spinning, all day long, while all these exciting things are going on. And catching a few flies. Even the flies, she says, aren't what they were in her young days—horrid skinny things, and half of 'em full of DDT." Mr. Webb laughed. "You know and I know, Freddy, that flies aren't any different. Never was much nourishment in 'em anyway. But you know how women are."

"Sure," said Freddy. "Well, have your gang

in here at four o'clock, eh? I'll tell you what we're going to do later."

Actually, Freddy had only the vaguest idea of what he was going to do. Harass Mr. Anderson, and try to drive him out of the hotel as he had driven Mrs. Filmore. But just how? Oh well, he could always think up seven different ways of doing something.

It was certainly an odd expedition that started from the farm at four o'clock. Freddy and Jinx and Georgie, a snake friend of Freddy's named Homer, the four mice, and a large flat carton lined with moss, containing the insect volunteers. Among these were Randolph, the beetle and his friend the thousand-legger, Jeffrey. Several wasps who were not needed to guard the rats, and Mr. and Mrs. Pomeroy, would join them next day.

Freddy and Jinx carried the carton between them. It was light, but it made hard going where the ground was rough. The Webbs rode in the carton to keep the volunteers in order. The mice rode on Georgie's back, and Homer was looped about his neck. Homer had been present on the occasion when the little girl visitor had made Georgie look silly by talking baby talk to him; and like a good many snakes, he thought that a good joke never wore out. He would coil himself affectionately around Georgie's neck, and then twist himself around in front until his nose was almost against Georgie's. "Who's um's ickle dolling pupsywups?" he would say in a little sickly-sweet voice, and kiss Georgie on the nose.

Every time he did this, the mice would get to giggling, and that would make Georgie even madder. He would snap at Homer, but the snake was too quick, and would dodge and then whip his coils so tight around the dog's neck that his eyes bulged. "I hug'm and kiss'm and hug'm and kiss'm," said Homer. Cousin Augustus giggled so hard he got the hiccups.

At Mr. Camphor's, while the canoe was being loaded, Freddy and Jinx went around to the porch. Miss Elmira was still there, and around her sat the three cows. They weren't saying anything. They just sat there, looking as mournful as possible. They stared at Miss Elmira with their great sad eyes, and every now and then one of them would give a low moo of despair. Charles was with them, his tailfeathers drooping, a small pocket handkerchief held to his eyes with one claw.

Miss Elmira too, of course, was draped and

enveloped in gloom, but Freddy thought she was looking a little impatient. He said to Bannister, who had come out and was looking over their shoulders: "Looks to me as if she was beginning to get enough."

The butler gave a faint sniffle. "Ah, sir," he said, "a great tragic actress was lost to the world when Mrs. Wiggins became a cow."

"Pooh," said Jinx; "she's good all right—I'll hand you that. But there's more to acting than just sitting still and mugging. An actor acts. You got to give 'em action. Watch me."

He walked over and stood between Mrs. Wiggins and Mrs. Wurzburger. "Ma'am," he said, "you may think you got trouble. You may think you got afflictions that make a monkey out of Job. But listen to me. A: my father was killed by a flatiron last week when he was conducting a backyard concert. B: my mother died of grief. C: my wife and seven children were tied up in a sack and drowned by a wicked butler." He began to pace up and down. "D: I've got rheumatism, hives and hay fever. E:—" Evidently he couldn't think of anything for E, for he sat down, lifted up his head, and began to wail.

There is no use trying to describe those wails.

Multiply any cat you've ever heard by ten, and add a few assorted owls, and you might get somewhere near it. They quavered and soared and broke into despairing gobblings, and then rose to a screech again. Mr. Camphor and Miss Minerva came rushing out. "What on *earth*!" Miss Minerva exclaimed. She looked at the circle of weeping animals about her sister. "Is it—is it something they had for lunch?"

"My goodness, I don't know where you could get anything for lunch, except maybe live scorpions, that would make them act that way," said Mr. Camphor.

Freddy explained to Miss Minerva what they were trying to do. But she shook her head. "You may be on the right track. We've always been very cheerful with her, and maybe being gloomy might change her. But even as a little girl she was like this. Used to give each of her dolls a handkerchief when she put them to bed, so they could cry in the night. She just wants to be miserable. She can walk around as well as I can, you know. She stays in the wheel chair because it makes her feel like an invalid. I guess having her around like that is what makes me so impatient with Jimson sometimes. I've felt I had to be so extra nice to her." She looked speculatively at her sister. "Well, you animals are so anxious to help, the least I can do is join in."

She took out her handkerchief and went over to her sister, wiping her eyes. "My poor Elmira," she said, "how fortunate that you are no longer alone in your sadness. What a blessing that there are others—many others—who are even more sorrowful and despondent than you are!"

"They are not!" snapped Miss Elmira. She had been getting more and more restless, and with the words she sat up in her chair.

"EE-e-eeyowl-er-owl!" wailed Jinx.

"When in Rome, do as the Romans do," said Bannister, and fell sobbing on Mr. Camphor's shoulder.

Miss Elmira stared around defiantly at the grief-stricken group. She seemed very much disturbed, and Freddy began to feel that Charles had been right. She had always held the center of the stage, as the hopelessly sad person who had to be deferred to and coddled. But now she was just one of the chorus, one among many, all of whom seemed more startlingly dismal than she was.

"She's not the queen bee any more," he

thought. "She's like sick people, who feel important because everybody else in the house waits on them, and then they go to a hospital where everybody is sick, and they don't like it." Then he was aware that she was beckoning to him.

"That swamp," she said when he went over to her. "Where is it?"

"You mean the swamp I wrote the poem about? Why, I guess I was thinking of the Great Dismal Swamp. It's in Virginia, isn't it?"

"Bannister," she said, "place reservation to nearest point."

"Yes, madam," said Bannister, taking out his notebook. "Bus from Centerboro to Rome, plane from Rome to nearest point touching the swamp. I'll look that up, madam."

Miss Elmira said: "I'll pack my bag," and got up and followed him as lightly and easily as if she'd been exercising regularly, instead of sitting for days on end in a wheel chair.

"Well, I'll be darned!" said Mr. Camphor.

"Good gracious," said Freddy, "do you think she can take a trip like that? You think she'll be all right?"

"Look at her," said Mr. Camphor. "In those shawls and with that expression, can't you see people falling over themselves to give her the best seat in the bus? Everybody will want to help the poor old lady. My goodness, next time I travel, I'm going to put on a long white beard and carry a cane, and then maybe I won't have to stand up half the way."

"You do really think she'll be all right, Jimson?" said Miss Minerva. "I've looked after her for so long . . ."

"Certainly I do. She'll get herself a little place on the edge of the swamp, and she'll be as happy as a toad in a mud puddle. Or as gloomy. Matter of fact, maybe she plans to go down there and work up an extra case of gloom and then come back and show us all up."

Miss Minerva looked out across the lake, and then up at the sky. "Dear me," she said, "I do believe the sun is going to come out."

"It does seem brighter," said Mr. Camphor, "but the clouds are just as heavy."

"What's brighter is that Miss Elmira's gone," Freddy said.

Chapter 17

Freddy hadn't wanted Miss Minerva to go camping with them. He thought it would be a bother to have to keep feeding her compliments all day long so she wouldn't be cranky. And he had an idea she might be bossy. But as a matter of fact she was no trouble at all. She not only did her full share of the work, but she turned out to be good company. Some people are like that; in a different setting they are different people. Of course he and Camphor kept up the compliments; they weren't taking any chances.

But though Miss Minerva was an experienced woodsman, and even went out with her hatchet and built and roofed her own lean-to shelter, she had what Freddy thought were pretty silly ideas about fixing things up. She decorated the camp. She had brought along a lot of ribbons and doodads, and she put little frills and bows on everything. There was a little red bow on the frying pan, and big splashy pink bows on the canoe paddles, and she even had Jinx wearing a very fancy plaid bow around his neck. Mr. Camphor said: "That's what they call the feminine touch." He smiled at the cat. "Makes you look quite chic and charming, Jinx; quite one of the ten best dressed cats of the social season."

"Aw, choke it off, will you?" said Jinx. "If she wasn't so handy with a hatchet, do you think I'd let her make a monkey out of me like this?"

"Yeah, I think you would," said Freddy. "Or was it some other cat I saw a little while ago admiring himself in Mr. Camphor's shaving mirror?"

Jinx stalked off angrily. But he didn't take off the bow.

The first night Freddy put the carton containing the bug volunteers in the shelter where he and Mr. Camphor slept. Or rather, where they tried to sleep. For the crickets sang and chirped and sawed away on their fiddles all night long. Mr. Camphor sat up finally and lit the candle. "Are you awake, Freddy?" he said.

"Well, what do you think?" said the pig, sitting up too.

"I think we've got to do something about this. Good heavens, don't those creatures ever go to bed?"

"I don't know much about the sleeping habits of bugs," Freddy said. "Let's talk to Webb."

He took the cover off the carton and Mr. Webb climbed out and crawled into his ear, but not so far that it would tickle, and said: "I'm sorry about this, Freddy. We've tried every way we know to keep 'em quiet, even threatened to eat them. Mother's about frantic. She tied up a couple of them so they couldn't fiddle, but the others just cut them loose."

"But what's it all about?" Freddy asked.

"Sort of a patriotic rally, I gather. One of 'em

started singing *The Night Before the Battle, Mother,* and they all chimed in. Now they're singing the *Bean Marching Song.*"

"Sounds like just a lot of chirping to me."

"Sure. To me too. Modern stuff, I guess. Why don't you souse 'em in the lake?"

"Well," said Freddy, "I had you hire the noisiest bugs I could think of for this job; I oughtn't to kick if they do what I expected them to do. I'll take the carton down and leave it under the canoe." So he did, and slept like a top the rest of the night.

Freddy had a good time in the next two days. It was fun camping. They explored the woods and the lake, and he practiced paddling, and found every hour of the day packed with a dozen new things to learn and interesting things to do. Of course the main reason he enjoyed it so much was because he had a comfortable place to sleep at night. Lots of inexperienced campers come back from a trip, red-eyed and worn out from lack of sleep, and looking as if they had been dragged backwards through a briar patch. Freddy was lucky in having Mr. Camphor to show him the right way to do things at the start.

The second day they went down to Lakeside

They explored the woods and the lake.

and looked around. Carpenters were repairing the porch, and Gormley's, the plumber's, truck was parked beside the road. A woman was shaking a dust mop from an upper window. They went back to camp without asking any questions. But the following morning at breakfast they heard someone coming down the trail, and Jinx and Georgie and Charles disappeared into the bushes as Mr. Anderson appeared. He walked up to them. "Good morning. Mr. Camphor, isn't it? I'm Anderson." Then he looked at Freddy, who no longer wore his disguise. "Haven't I seen you before?"

"Very likely," said Freddy. "I'm around Centerboro a lot." And he thought: "He knows I'm after him, but he isn't sure whether or not I know he's Mr. Eha."

"This is Freddy, the well-known detective," said Mr. Camphor. "And my aunt, Miss Minerva Camphor."

Mr. Anderson bowed, but turned again to Freddy. "The detective?" he said. "Oh yes. Must be interesting work. Following people and peeking through keyholes and listening behind doors. Though I wouldn't care for such sneaky work myself." He laughed with false heartiness.

"He's trying to make me mad so I'll give myself away," Freddy thought. But two could play that game. He said calmly: "I doubt if you'd be much good at it. You're a pretty big man. You'd be always tripping and falling over things." He grinned at Mr. Anderson. "You probably lose your temper pretty easily too, don't you?"

Mr. Anderson's face got darker red, and he glared, breathing hard through his nose. But Mr. Camphor said: "Sit down. Sit down and have a flapjack. You'll like them, I think, if you've never tried one of my flapjacks."

Freddy thought for a minute that Mr. Anderson was going to burst into small pieces; for the ghost, of course, had not only tried one of Mr. Camphor's flapjacks, he had wrestled with one. But he controlled himself. Evidently he felt certain that they didn't know that he was Eha. "Thank you," he growled and sat down. Freddy noted with pleasure that he sat down very slowly and carefully, on account of birdshot.

"I understand," said Miss Minerva, "that you've bought Lakeside. My sister and I spent many pleasant summers there. What has become of dear Mrs. Filmore?"

Mr. Anderson had managed to choke back

his rage. "A great pity," he said. "She couldn't make a go of it. I didn't buy it myself, though. I am merely acting for a group of New York capitalists—getting it in shape to open. Next month, we hope. I trust that you and your sister will stay with us again?"

"We plan to," said Miss Minerva with an odd smile. "Though I suppose you won't be there?"

"Oh, yes, I moved up last night; I shall be there from now on."

He ate several flapjacks and they talked of this and that. Freddy didn't needle him any more, and after a while he got up and went back to Lakeside.

"He didn't find out much," said Mr. Camphor. "But we didn't accomplish anything either."

"Oh, yes we did," said Freddy. "The Webbs are riding back to the hotel on his coat collar. Now we've got spies right in the enemy's camp."

The day was spent in planning and preparation, and that evening, as soon as it got dark, Freddy left Mr. Camphor and Miss Minerva beside the campfire and moved his forces up. With Jinx scouting in advance, they carried the box containing the bug allies up the trail as far as the edge of the Lakeside lawn. From there the bugs proceeded on foot, under the leadership of the head cricket, up to the porch, where Mr. and Mrs. Webb were to take charge. Homer and the four mice went with them, but the others stayed back among the trees.

The carpenters and plumbers had gone home at five o'clock, but Mr. Anderson's car stood on the lawn with another old car beside it. There were lights in two of the upper hotel windows. Nothing happened for a while, and then Freddy saw a very faint and tiny glow of light coming towards him through the grass. It didn't come in a straight line, but wavered from side to side, and as it came closer he saw that it was Homer, with a firefly on his head to light the way. Beside the firefly stood a spider, and Freddy could see that they were hanging on by a strand of web that was looped like a bridle around the snake's neck.

"Boy, was that firefly a good idea, Freddy!" said Homer. "Just like having headlights. I can travel twice as fast at night."

"Well, you'll travel without me next time," said Mrs. Webb tartly, and climbed shakily up on Freddy's nose. "If anybody ever invites you to go snake-back riding, Freddy, you just politely excuse yourself. That canoe ride over here was bad enough, but this was ten times worse. Why any mortal creature can't go from one place to another in a straight line, instead of dodging and zigzagging all over creation, beats me!"

"Now, now, Mother Webb," said Homer, "lots of folks pay good money to get a ride like that on roller coasters at amusement parks." He glided over to Georgie and began teasing him with baby talk.

Mrs. Webb snorted. It was a pretty small snort, of course, but very expressive. Then she gave Freddy her report.

Mr. Anderson was not alone in the hotel. He had brought a couple named Jones up from Centerboro to help get the place in shape, and later to act as handy man and housekeeper. The old car was theirs, and they had the lighted room in the back. Mr. Anderson's was the front one.

"Mr. Webb is getting the crickets placed now," she said, "in cracks and keyholes and safe places where they can't be caught. They'll start in as soon as the lights are out. That's all you're going to do tonight, isn't it?"

"That ought to be enough for Anderson tonight," Freddy said. "We just want to wear him down by keeping him awake. But those Joneses—can anybody get into their room?"

"The mice were going to gnaw holes in both rooms, so we could all get in and out easily."

"They'd better do that tomorrow in the daytime, when nobody'll hear them," said Freddy. "We'll just try crickets tonight, to see how it works. Homer had better go back and help keep an eye on things, but since that ride over here made you seasick, you might as well stay here."

"No, no; I'll go back," said the spider. "I don't like to leave Father alone. He's right in Anderson's room, under the bed. And he's got one or two ideas I'd just as soon he didn't try out. You know how daring he is. He'll be more careful if I'm there." So pretty soon she and the firefly got on Homer's head and started out.

After a few minutes the light in the Joneses' room went out, and then Mr. Anderson's window was put up. They saw him lean out and look at the night, then he disappeared and his light went out too. And immediately through the stillness came the chirp of a cricket. Another joined in, and then another, until pretty soon the whole night seemed to be full of their singing. "Golly," said Freddy in an awed tone, "I bet you can hear them halfway across the lake."

After about five minutes of it the lights went on again in both rooms—and every sound was cut off short. Shadows moved across the lights, and Mr. Anderson's window went down with a bang. The lights went out . . . and the crickets started fiddling.

Four times this happened, and each time the lights were left on longer. "They're trying to find the crickets," Freddy said. "I hope Webb found safe places for them. You know what Anderson will do if he finds one."

"I know what I'd do," said Georgie.

"Remember how we yelled under old Witherspoon's window that night, to keep him awake?" said Jinx.

"That's what gave me the idea," Freddy said. "Only we've got to do a lot more to Anderson before we get through. We've got to make him mad. We've got to make him so mad he'll begin doing foolish things. Then we'll have him."

"You mean," said Charles, "that that's the only idea you've got for getting rid of him?"

"Sure," said Freddy. "Why?"

"Well, it's the silliest thing I ever heard of!" said the rooster.

"Is it? Remember the time you got so mad at a truck driver for calling you a chicken that you'd have let him run over you before you'd get out of the road?"

"Pooh, it isn't the same thing at all!" said Charles.

"All right. You wait and see. —Hey, there go the lights again. Hear 'em banging around! They're getting pretty mad already."

There had been several thumps and a crash in Mr. Anderson's room, followed by a lot of bad language. At least it sounded like the worst kind of language, though they couldn't hear the words. Then things quieted down, but the lights were left on.

Of course crickets are annoyed by sudden light, and prefer to sing in the dark, but these crickets had their orders, and after a minute, realizing that the lights weren't going to be put out again, the full chorus started up again.

"I can't stand this," said Georgie. "I guess I've got a sympathetic nature. I keep thinking what it's like for that poor man in there until I'm just about as nervous as he is. I'm going back to camp."

"I suppose we might as well all go back and get some sleep," said Freddy. "Webb will keep things rolling until daylight, and Homer and the mice will be there."

"Well, my nature's not sympathetic," Jinx said, "and I wouldn't miss this for eight pounds of prime catnip. If the guy goes crazy I want to be here to see. Go on. I'll keep an eye on things."

Miss Minerva and Mr. Camphor were rolled up in their sleeping bags, and the fire had burned down. Mr. Camphor wasn't snoring. "Thoughtful of his aunt, even in his sleep," Freddy said to himself. He crawled into his lean-to and was asleep also in two minutes.

When he awoke it was broad daylight, and the Camphors were getting breakfast. Jinx strolled up as Freddy came out from his plunge in the lake. "Boy, did you miss a show!" he said. "Those crickets sure can keep up the chatter—they ought to be in Congress. Old Anderson never slept a wink, and finally, about an hour before daylight, he really cut loose. He yelled and smashed things—I bet there isn't a whole stick of furniture left in that room."

"How about the Joneses?"

"They quit about three. Piled in their car,

after a yelling match with the boss. Boy, has that Mrs. Jones got a rough tongue—she filed Anderson down to about three inches high. Finally he said he'd get some DDT and spray the place in the morning, but they said he could put it in the bathtub and drown himself in it if he wanted to—they were through. And off they went."

"DDT!" said Freddy. "I don't like that. Spiders don't mind it, but I don't know about crickets. We'll have to give that a little thought."

"I've arranged to get hourly reports of what goes on from the mice," Jinx said. "One of them, or Homer, will meet one of us every hour on the hour, under that big beech at the edge of the hotel lawn. Right now Brother Anderson is making up a little of his lost sleep. On a settee in the lounge."

"We can't have that," said Freddy. "What's the matter with the crickets?"

"They knocked off at six-thirty. Said they'd only work an eight hour night."

"My goodness," Freddy said, "this is a war; they're not working in a factory!"

"Yeah, Webb had an argument with them about that. They claim it's the same as any orchestra, and they're working under musicians' union rules. You'd better let 'em alone or you'll have a strike on your hands. Anyway, Webb's there; I don't guess Anderson'll get much sleep."

"What can Mr. Webb do?"

"What can he do!" Jinx exclaimed. "Say, you ought to see it. Why don't you go pay Anderson a little call? Just go to the door of the lounge and look in. You can make some excuse —tell him you want to borrow a cup of flour or something. Come on—it's worth it."

Freddy hesitated, but he didn't think that Mr. Anderson would dare do anything more than possibly order him out, so he and Jinx walked down to the hotel. They went quietly up on the porch and looked into the lounge. Mr. Anderson lay on his back on the settee, asleep with his mouth open. Freddy looked inquiringly at Jinx, and the cat pointed up at the ceiling, where he saw two little black spots. Then they moved, and he realized that it was the Webbs.

As he watched, Mr. Webb spun down on a long strand directly above Mr. Anderson's face. Halfway down he stopped and waved a couple of legs at Freddy, then went on and anchored the strand cautiously to the man's left ear. At the same time Mrs. Webb ran a line down to his right ear, and then between the two lines, and just an inch or two above his face, they wove a web. They worked fast, and when the web was finished, they ran swiftly up to the ceiling and cut the two lines loose, so that the whole web dropped down across the sleeper's face.

Mr. Anderson's nose wiggled, his eyelids twitched, and then as the web settled closer across his mouth, he woke with a sort of snarl and started up, clawing at his face.

"Good morning," said Freddy pleasantly.

Mr. Anderson swung round, still brushing at the cobweb. "You!" he said. "What are you doing here?"

"Me?" said Freddy. "Nothing. I was just taking a walk and I thought I'd drop in. Sorry if I woke you. I hope you slept well, your first night in Lakeside?"

Three seconds later the two animals were tearing up the trail towards camp, followed by the infuriated roars of Mr. Anderson and also by several stones, which whizzed and clipped through the foliage above them.

"I wonder what upset him so?" said Freddy

when they slowed down out of range.

"I can't imagine," said Jinx. "Maybe he didn't sleep well."

Then they both burst out laughing.

"Just the same," said Jinx, "you'd better not pull that one again. If he's that mad after one night, what'll he be in a week?"

"That's what I want to find out," said Freddy.

Chapter 18

The Camphors were at breakfast, and Freddy and Jinx joined them. Georgie had finished and gone for a swim in the lake. "I warned him he oughtn't to swim on a full stomach," said Miss Minerva, "but he was rather impertinent to me, so I didn't insist."

Mr. Camphor laughed. "What Georgie said was that it depended on what your stomach was full of. He said he realized that with six of Aunt's flapjacks inside him he'd probably sink before he took two strokes, but he'd take one of the cork canoe cushions to hold him up. He was just trying to be funny, Aunt."

"I wasn't angry," she said. "What's bothering me is these wasps. There's one on the edge of your plate now, Freddy."

"Oh, don't worry about him," Freddy said. "He's come to help us. Hello, Jake. You missed a lot of excitement last night."

"That doesn't bother me," said the wasp. "I can always stir up a little of my own if I feel the need of it. Where's this guy you want punctured?"

"He's up at the hotel. Big red-faced man— you can't miss him. I think you and the boys better go bother him a little—you know our plan—but don't sting him yet. We're saving that for later."

At half-past eight the plumbers and carpenters came back, and after that there was so much hammering and sawing and banging on pipes that Freddy knew Mr. Anderson wouldn't get much sleep. But what about the DDT? They could put his car out of commission so he couldn't drive to town for it himself, but he'd only ask the carpenters to bring him a bottle of it.

It was Miss Minerva who solved that problem. And when, at eleven o'clock, the mice reported that Mr. Anderson had started for Centerboro, she said: "You leave it to me. Jimson, I'll need your help. Come along." And they started down to Lakeside.

When Mr. Anderson came back an hour or so later, he got out of his car to find Miss Minerva lying at the foot of the porch steps, groaning.

"Well, ma'am, what are you doing here?" he asked unsympathetically.

"Oh dear, oh dear," Miss Minerva moaned; "it's my ankle. I fell off the porch. I called and called, but the workmen are all inside eating their lunch and they didn't hear me."

"I guess you didn't call very loud," said Mr. Anderson. "Well, what do you want me to do?"

"Want you to do!" she snapped. "I want you to pick me up—help me back to camp. What sort of man are you anyway, when you see a lady in trouble, to stand there and ask questions?"

"I'm a very busy man," he replied. "You had no business on my porch in the first place. I'll send one of the men for your nephew."

Miss Minerva didn't want that at all. "You'll help me yourself—*now*," she said. "Or I'll sue you for damages. This porch is unsafe and I can prove it."

It probably occurred to Mr. Anderson that to have to defend a lawsuit against a former guest wasn't the best way to open a hotel season. "Very well," he said grudgingly, and put down his packages on the porch.

Mr. Camphor, hiding behind a bush, watched them start up the path. Mr. Anderson's arm was about Miss Minerva's waist, and hers was about his neck, as she hobbled along, leaning heavily on him. "Looks like Lovers' Lane," said Mr. Camphor sentimentally. Then as they disappeared, he came out, picked up the bottle of DDT and poured the contents out on the ground, after which he took it down and filled it with lake water. When Mr. Anderson came back a little later he carried the bottle into the hotel.

The hourly reports from the mice were as follows: One o'clock: Mr. Anderson spraying room. Two o'clock: After giving the carpenters some instructions, Mr. Anderson lay down for a nap, but was disturbed by wasps, which kept zooming down at him from the ceiling, then flying away before he could swat them. Three o'clock: Mr. Anderson still awake. Tried to smoke, but crickets had chewed holes in the sides of his cigars so they wouldn't draw. Four o'clock: A Mr. and Mrs. Edipus came from Centerboro to take the place of the Joneses. Mr. Anderson told them what they were expected to do, then went for a walk in the woods. We have now lost contact with the enemy.

So Freddy sent the wasps to reconnoiter, and presently they came back to report that Mr. Anderson was lying down asleep under a tree. "Shall we poke him up a little?" Jacob asked.

"You save your stings till he's so sound asleep we can't wake him any other way," Freddy said. "Georgie, where are those squirrels who were around begging for cold flapjacks this morning? Get hold of them, will you?"

So Georgie rounded up the squirrels, and Freddy made a deal with them. They took some small stones in their cheek pouches, and went up in the tree under which Mr. Anderson was asleep—with his mouth open, as usual. They got on a branch right over his head and tried to drop the stones in his mouth.

Squirrels are pretty good at this. The first two stones hit Mr. Anderson's chest and only made him grumble a little, but the third one was a bull's-eye, and he gave a gulp and started up to glare wildly around and wonder what it

Squirrels are pretty good at this.

was that he had swallowed, and that he could still feel going down. Then he looked up and saw the squirrels. He yelled at them and shook his fist, but squirrels just think that kind of thing is funny; they chattered back mockingly, so he got up wearily and went in search of another tree. And the squirrels followed him.

After about an hour of this Mr. Anderson went back to the hotel. The workmen had gone, and the mice reported at six o'clock that Mrs. Edipus was cooking supper. At seven, Mr. Anderson went to bed, giving the Edipuses strict orders that he was not to be disturbed. At seven-five the crickets tuned up.

Jinx kept watch again that night. "I wouldn't miss it for eight pounds of prime catnip *and* two quarts of cream," he said. "I haven't had so much fun since Mrs. Wiggins fell out of the swing." The others went to bed, but about one in the morning Jinx waked them up. "Anderson just came out and got in his car and drove off," he said. "He's probably gone home to Centerboro to get a good night's sleep in his own bed."

"Good gracious, that'll spoil all the good work we've done," said Freddy. "How about the Edipuses?"

"Oh, they weren't as tough as the Joneses. They left at midnight."

Mr. Camphor crawled out of his sleeping bag. "I know what we can do," he said. "Come on, Freddy. Aunt Minerva, you build up the fire—big, big, so it looks like a house burning up from off Centerboro way." Without explaining further, he ran down and he and Freddy got into the canoe and paddled across to his house. "We don't really need to hurry," he said. "It'll take Anderson half an hour to get home and we'll allow about twenty minutes more for him to get to bed and asleep, before we phone. It'll make him madder if we wake him up than if we catch him just as he gets in."

They went up to the house and roused Bannister, and Mr. Camphor gave him his instructions. Then, when they figured Mr. Anderson had had time to get to bed, Bannister phoned.

He had to ring about twenty times, but at last Mr. Anderson answered.

"Sorry to bother you, sir," said Bannister. "This is Mr. Camphor's butler, up at the lake. There's a big fire over on the north shore—looks like a house burning. I understand you've bought Lakeside, and I thought. . . . Oh no, sir; I've never seen a campfire as big as that, and Mr. Camphor and his friends should be asleep at this hour. . . . I can't see, sir; Mr. Camphor has our telescope with him. It's right in the direction of Lakeside. . . . No sir, I didn't call the fire department; I thought I should call you first. . . . Yes sir? Thank you, sir." And Bannister hung up.

"Well, Bannister—thanks," said Mr. Camphor. "We'll have to get back. Anything new?"

"No, sir. Miss Elmira got off safely this morning. Very quiet day, sir. Very pleasant."

"Good. Come along, Freddy."

Miss Minerva had certainly built up a real fire. The flames leaped to treetop height, and the glare must have been visible for miles. The canoe was almost back to the camp when Freddy heard in the distance the faint wail of a siren. "They'll have seen the glow by this time," said Mr. Camphor as they beached the canoe. "Well, let's pull it apart a little, and get into our bags."

Ten minutes later, when the fire truck came roaring and shrieking and bounding down the rough road and pulled up beside the hotel, the fire had sunk down, and everyone in the camp was apparently asleep. Everyone except Freddy and Jinx, who had circled around through the woods back of the hotel, and were hiding behind a shed near the end of the road.

The firemen piled off the truck, whose searchlight was playing over the front of the building. Then Mr. Anderson drove up behind them, and they surrounded him in an angry group, demanding to know why they had been pulled out of bed when there wasn't any fire.

"You saw it yourselves," he protested. "The sky was all red."

There was plenty of argument back and forth, and then the firemen called Mr. Anderson a lot of names and piled on the truck and drove roaring and shrieking and bounding home.

As soon as Mr. Anderson went indoors, Freddy came out of hiding. Very cautiously he lifted the hood of the car, disconnected all the wires he could reach, unscrewed everything unscrewable and loosened everything loosenable, and then went back to camp.

Chapter 19

Jinx's report at breakfast time was a very favorable one. Mr. Anderson had tried to take a nap in the lounge, but the cricket treatment soon drove him out. He went to his car and tried for half an hour to get it started. Then he looked under the hood. "And I never heard anybody say such things about anybody as he did about you, Freddy," said Jinx. "He's pretty sure you did it. And he's coming down here this morning. You'd better be ready to duck."

"We'll be ready for him," said Freddy.

"What happened after he gave up trying to start the car?"

"He was so sleepy that he could hardly stand up. He stumbled around and sort of collapsed in one of the chairs on the porch. The crickets were hollering good, but I guess he was so tired that he went to sleep anyway." Jinx grinned maliciously. "He looked real cute—so sort of innocent and unprotected—I thought maybe if I sang him a little lullaby, he'd rest better. Wow! He like to went through the ceiling! Of course I was pretty close to his ear—I didn't want him to miss any of my clear, bell-like tones.

"So then he staggered in to get his pistol. But Homer and the mice found it in a drawer yesterday, and they also found an open pot of glue the carpenter had been repairing something with. So they sort of put two and two together, and poured the glue over the pistol." Jinx laughed again. "Anderson felt in the drawer and got his hand on the pistol all right, but it took him ten minutes and practically his entire vocabulary to get it off again. The glue had only partly set."

"Golly!" said Freddy. "What an awful night! I feel sorry for the poor man."

"Well, I don't," said the cat. "Don't forget, he was going to cheat us out of our homes, just as he did poor Mrs. Filmore, and make beggars of us all. And all we've done is cheat him out of a couple nights' sleep. But you've got to let Jacob take over now—noise won't keep him awake much longer."

"Where is he now?" Mr. Camphor asked.

"Wandering around, here and there. He's so groggy that even the mice and Homer aren't afraid of him. Eek nipped his ear once and woke him, and then when he dropped off again, Homer kind of slithered over his face. Boy, that got results! I don't think he likes snakes. He's out in the woods somewhere, but the squirrels are keeping up the good work."

"I think I hear him coming now," said Miss Minerva. And sure enough, up the path came Mr. Anderson. He stopped a little way off, leaning with one hand against a tree, and with his head thrust forward peered vaguely at them with red-rimmed eyes. He looked completely exhausted.

"Good morning, Mr. Anderson; lovely day, isn't it?" said Mr. Camphor.

Mr. Anderson clenched his fists. He pulled himself together and strode towards them.

"You, pig," he said thickly to Freddy. "What did you do to my car?"

Freddy glanced inquiringly at Mr. Camphor, and Mr. Camphor nodded slightly. Their look said that they were agreed that the time had come for a showdown. For they both knew that although their plan had been to get him so mad that he would do something completely foolish, he was really too exhausted to be mad now. Indeed, they could use his exhaustion better than they could perhaps have used his anger.

Freddy stood up. "I disconnected a lot of things," he said boldly. "Why?"

"Why? Why?" Mr. Anderson shouted hoarsely. "Because I'm going to put you where you belong—behind prison bars, that's why."

"How are you going to prove I did it?" Freddy asked. "Fingerprints? But I haven't got fingers—only trotters." He held them up.

"You've admitted it in front of witnesses," said Mr. Anderson. "I guess that will be enough proof."

"But only," Miss Minerva said, "if the witnesses heard him say it. We didn't hear anything like that, did we, Jimson?"

"Certainly not," said Mr. Camphor.

"So that's the way it is," said Mr. Anderson. "You're all in it together."

"That's it," Mr. Camphor said. "Quite illegal. If you can prove it. Just as your scheme to get this hotel, and later to get my house and the Bean farm, was quite illegal. We couldn't prove it either. But now your rats have been driven off, your ghost scheme has exploded, and it's our turn. How do you like it?"

And then Mr. Anderson's temper flared up and his self-control, weakened by lack of sleep, vanished entirely. "I'll show you how I like it!" he roared, and started for Mr. Camphor.

But Miss Minerva, who had been scrubbing out the frying pan, got up and stood in his way.

"One side, woman!" he shouted. "I wouldn't like to strike a lady."

"I wouldn't like to strike a gentleman," said Miss Minerva. "But I guess there's no danger of that." And as he tried to brush past her, she lifted the frying pan and brought it down with a loud dong! on the top of his head.

At another time the blow wouldn't have bothered Mr. Anderson much. But his head was already swimming with exhaustion, and the shock of it was just enough to make him

She lifted the frying pan and brought it down with a loud dong!

completely dizzy. He staggered, turned half round, then fell flat on his face.

"Dear me!" said Miss Minerva. She looked with surprise at the frying pan, then set it down gingerly on the ground. Mr. Anderson shook his head two or three times, then got slowly to his feet.

"You'll regret this, ma'am," he said. "You'll regret it all your life."

"Yes," she said, "I expect I shall. I'll regret that I didn't hit harder."

"Sit down, Anderson," said Mr. Camphor sternly. "I'll get you some coffee. We want to have a talk with you."

"Well, I don't want to talk with you," Mr. Anderson said. "Why, confound you, you silly little red-headed donkey, do you think you're going to make any terms with me? I'll smash you . . ." He stopped abruptly, as Miss Minerva again picked up the frying pan.

"Yes, I think we can make terms with you," said Mr. Camphor. "Listen to me. We have prepared a paper here, and you are going to sign it."

"Huh, don't make me laugh!" said Mr. Anderson.

"We're not trying to. We're just trying to

see that you don't sleep until you've signed.
You know that you won't get any sleep here at
Lakeside. But I suppose you think that you can
spend your nights in your home in Centerboro. So you can. But you won't sleep there
either. We have by no means exhausted all our
methods for keeping people awake. Crickets
can get into your house as easily as into this
hotel. And there are doorbells that can ring,
telephone bells in the middle of the night, mice
gnawing in the woodwork—we have a hundred
means at our disposal.—Here, wake up!" For
Mr. Anderson's head had fallen forward on his
chest.

"You have a very soothing voice, Mr. Camphor," said Freddy. And then as Mr. Anderson
gave a long comfortable snore: "Hi, Jacob!"
he called.

There was a droning buzz, and the wasp lit
on Mr. Anderson's collar. "Thanks, pal," he
said. "Where do you want me to begin drilling
—you got any preference?"

"You pick your own spot."

Jacob took out his sting and polished it on
the coat collar, then walked up onto Mr. Anderson's neck and looked around with a pro-
fessional air. "I always like this spot just below

the ear," he said. "The nose is more spectac-
ular, but in the long run the neck gives the
best results. Well, here we go!" And he drove
the sting in.

The results indeed were excellent. Mr. Anderson's snore turned into a screech, and he
leaped up, clawing at his neck. He danced
around for a moment wildly, then clasping his
neck in both hands, dropped down on a log
and stared up at them balefully under drooping eyelids.

"You see," said Mr. Camphor pleasantly,
"no signature, no sleep." He held out a paper,
and after a moment Mr. Anderson took it with
a grunt and started to read. Halfway through
he started up. "Do you think I'm crazy?" he
said. "Why, this thing—you could jail me on it
any time you wanted to!"

"Quite right," said Mr. Camphor. "But we
won't if you behave yourself. We will give it
back to you when you have given the hotel you
stole back to Mrs. Filmore."

"Oh, yeah?" Mr. Anderson's face twisted in
an unpleasant sneer. His whole expression now
betrayed how dishonest he really was, for he
was too tired to keep on playing the part of the
bluff, genial good fellow whom most Center-

boro people thought him. "Give it back, eh?
I paid good money for that hotel, and . . ."

"And Mrs. Filmore will pay it back to you,"
Mr. Camphor interrupted, "less, of course,
what it costs to repair the damage you have
done. Say three thousand dollars."

Mr. Anderson was again peering at the paper. "Listen to this," he said. "'I confess that I
did feloniously, and with malice aforethought,
scare, frighten and terrify the employees of said
hotel, to the end that they might, and subse-
quently, did, flee in terror and consternation;
and that I furthermore, in pursuance of my
criminal and iniquitous machinations . . .'
Why, I don't even know what it means!"

Mr. Camphor smiled a self-satisfied smile.
"I thought I worded it rather well," he said.
"Hey!" Mr. Anderson's head had begun to
droop again. Mr. Camphor seized his shoulder
and shook it. "Wake up! Sign this paper!"

Mr. Anderson roused slightly, and held out
a groping hand for the pen Mr. Camphor put
into it. He signed, then fell right off the log
onto his back and went to sleep.

Mr. Camphor tucked a copy of the paper
into the sleeper's pocket, with a note at the bottom saying that the original would be turned

over to the district attorney within three days unless Mrs. Filmore had bought back Lakeside for three thousand dollars. "That'll fix it," Mr. Camphor said. "He'll know, when he wakes up and looks at the paper, that he's got to return the hotel or go to jail."

"It didn't take long to break him down," said Freddy. "I thought we'd have to keep him awake for a week."

"Those big men!" said Mr. Camphor complacently. "They can't take it."

"Nonsense!" said Miss Minerva. "He broke down because he knew he had done a wicked thing. If he'd been in the right, you'd never have got him to sign." She looked down at Mr. Anderson, who was sleeping as peacefully as a baby, with his head in the ashes of last night's fire. The ashes blew up in little grey clouds as he breathed. "What are we going to do with him?"

"Let's get the carpenters to take him home," said Freddy. "We don't want him here, cluttering up the scenery, any longer. Where's the carton?—I'll have to round up the bugs and take them and Homer and the mice back to the farm. And then . . ." He hesitated. "Well, are we going to break up camp now?" He looked around regretfully at the shelters and the beach and the fireplace.

"Why should we?" said Mr. Camphor. "We haven't had much fun yet on our camping trip."

"I don't want to go home yet," said Miss Minerva.

"Oh, that's wonderful," said Freddy. "Then if Bannister can drive us down to the farm, I can come back again."

Mr. Bean looked curiously at Freddy when Bannister drove the animals into the barnyard. It was plain that he was anxious to know what had happened, but it was against his principles to ask any animal questions. Freddy explained this to Bannister, so the butler brought Mr. Bean up to date, while Freddy ran off to tell Mrs. Wiggins.

Mrs. Wiggins and her sisters were delighted, but they had one disquieting bit of news: the rats had escaped during the night. However, Uncle Solomon had sighted them shortly before midnight, traveling steadily south. "I don't think we have to worry about them, Freddy," said the cow. "They couldn't do anything alone against us. I don't believe we'll ever see them again."

Freddy said he hoped so and went back to the waiting car. Mr. Bean was leaning on the car door, talking to Bannister. Beside him on the ground were several cartons and a large package. When Freddy came up, he reached out and patted the pig's head. "This pig, Bannister," he said, "is a fine pig. Mrs. Bean and I are very fond of this pig. He's smart as a whiplash, Bannister. Going camping with Mr. Camphor, you tell me. Well, I was down to Centerboro yesterday, and I saw some things in the Busy Bee I thought might be good for him to have. Couldn't figure out which one he'd like best, so I bought the whole kit and bilin'. You can just heave 'em in the back, there."

"Oh, Mr. Bean!" Freddy began. But Mr. Bean turned his back on him and said to Bannister: "Get along with you now." And he walked into the house.

Back in camp again Freddy undid the packages. The big package was a tent, just like the one the rats had destroyed. In the cartons was everything imaginable for camping—nested cooking utensils, a small axe, a little pressure kerosene stove, a compass, a hunting knife in a sheath, a camera, a pair of binoculars—everything anyone could possibly want.

One day about two weeks later, Miss Minerva and Freddy were out fishing in the canoe. Mr. Camphor had gone to Lakeside to help Mrs. Filmore hang curtains—the hotel was to open the first of June. The camp had now taken on the look of a permanent camp, for Mr. Camphor had decided that he liked living there better than he did in his big house across the lake. Miss Minerva, who now required only two compliments a day—three on rainy days—to keep her from getting cross, agreed that she liked it better too, though later in the season she might stay for a while at Lakeside, where she had spent so many happy summers. Even Bannister had finally come over to stay. Mr. Camphor hadn't wanted him at first; he said that he didn't need dignity out in the woods. But when Bannister agreed to be as undignified as possible while in camp, Mr. Camphor let him come.

Today Bannister had paddled over to get the mail and some supplies. Miss Minerva had just landed a good-sized perch, and Freddy was taking it off the hook for her, when he looked up and saw the butler's canoe approaching. He wasn't surprised to see Jinx sitting up in the bow. One or other of the farm animals was al-

ways coming up to spend a day or two. But this
time Jinx called out to him: "Come ashore.
I've got a message for you."

It was a letter that the cat had, and this is
what it said:

Mr. Frederick Bean
Pres. First Animal Bank of Centerboro
Editor Bean Home News
Stony Point, Jones's Bay, Lake Otesaraga 45,
    N. Y.

Dear Sir:

At a meeting of the depositors of the First
Animal Bank, it was unanimously agreed to
pass a vote of censure, directed against you, for
neglecting your financial duties by closing the
First Animal Bank without warning, and keeping it closed for three weeks, to the great detri-
ment and disgust of said depositors.

It was further agreed, that in the event you
do not return pronto, the Committee for the
Depositors will combine to form an independent bank, to be known as the Bean Trust &
Fidelity Co., and will endeavor by all the means
in their power to take your banking business
away from you. This they will undoubtedly be
able to accomplish, as everybody is sick of waiting for you to come back.

At a later meeting of the subscribers to the
Bean Home News, a vote of censure was pro-

posed and passed against you, for the neglect of editorial duties, in that no issue of the Bean Home News has appeared for three weeks. A committee, headed by Mr. J. J. Pomeroy, is now drafting plans for an independent newspaper, to be known as the Rural Animal Intelligencer, which will be written entirely in verse, ("Huh," said Freddy, "J.J.'s two lines of poetry is going to his head!") and will be distributed free.

Yours faithfully,

J. J. Pomeroy

JJP/JJP   For the Committee

"Well, I'll be darned!" said Freddy. "Written on my own typewriter, too! What's there to this, Jinx? Are they really sore?"

"Oh, not really. But it is a nuisance not having the bank open. Hank and I wanted to go to the movies night before last, and Hank had to borrow the money from Mrs. Bean. Quite upset him—you know how shy he is."

"I suppose you couldn't have borrowed it?"

"Sure I could have! But I've taken Hank three or four times, and has he ever taken me once?—he has not! I just told him it was time he did something about it."

Freddy said: "Well, to get back to this letter, who wrote it?"

"Charles drafted it. Lot of nice words in it, aren't there?"

"I thought I recognized his fine Italian claw," said Freddy.

"Written in Italian, eh?" said Jinx. "Guess that's why I couldn't understand more than half of it. Oh sure, I read it on the way over— I knew you wouldn't mind. Here's a word now: censure. What's that mean?"

"I don't know exactly," said Freddy. "I guess it means—oh, I don't know, I guess a vote of censure is the opposite of three loud cheers. Well, I'd better go down."

Mr. Camphor, who had come back from Lakeside and was sitting on a log looking at his mail, now called to Freddy: "Hey, look at this."

It was a picture postcard, a photograph of a little tumbledown hut which stood on the edge of a muddy looking stream. All about stood huge forbidding looking trees, their branches draped in tattered black rags of moss. Everything looked damp. There were two alligators on the mud bank beside the house. And written under it were these words: "Having a terrible time. Glad you are not here. Everything awful. Very happy. Your loving Aunt Elmira."

"Can you beat it?" said Mr. Camphor. "We

did everything possible for her; talked cheerfully to her, waited on her—and she goes and lives in a swamp!"

"I've been thinking about that," said Freddy. "You were nice to her, all right. But being nice to people—well, I guess it's giving them what *they* want, instead of what we think they *ought* to want."

"Yeah," said Jinx. "Well, the boys want the bank open. How about it, pig?"

So Freddy said goodbye to the Camphors and promised to come back for a day or two anyway, and maybe longer, as soon as he'd got things straightened out at home. Then he and Bannister and Jinx set out in the canoe.

Freddy looked back mournfully at the camp, as it got gradually smaller and smaller. "On the road to Jones's Bay," he thought. "It is—it is always bright and gay. No—no good." Then he thought: "Gracious, if I've got to get out an issue of the paper tomorrow, I'd better get busy. Let's see, there ought to be a poem; maybe another one in the series about the features. H'm." He got out his notebook.

And as always, in the pleasure of composition, he forgot his sadness. This is what he wrote:

THE FEATURES, NO. 5
THE EARS

The ears are two in number, and
Beside the head, on either hand,—
One to the left, one to the right—
They are attached extremely tight.
Their purpose is twofold, to wit:
To give the hat a place to sit,
So that it will not lose its place
And, slipping down, engulf the face.
Also to ventilate the brain,
When heated by great mental strain,
By standing at right angles out
To catch whatever wind's about,
Or when the summer breeze is napping,
To substitute by gently flapping.
Do not, therefore, attempt to pull
The ears from off the parent skull.
Though ears look odd and out of place,
And add so little to the face,
Though as adornment they're lamentable,
Without them you'd be unpresentable;
And he who rashly grabs the shears
Will find too late, with bitter tears,
That there's no substitute for ears.

"There," said Freddy. "My goodness, it's nice to get back into harness again."